NIGHT SHADE

NIGHTGARDEN SAGA #7

LUCY HOLDEN

FEHU PRESS

For Mackinley Messenger
Who has magic
That is all her own.

THE NIGHTGARDEN SAGA IN ORDER

Book #1: Red Magnolia
Book #2: Moonvine
Book #3: Poison Berry
Book #4: Bayou Rose
Book #5: Dusky Dahlia
Book #6: Blue Lilies
Book #7: Night Shade

There is also a prequel, told from Antoine's perspective, available on my website. Go to www.paulaconstant.com to download.

SET IN THE SAME WORLD

Fleur de Lis
The Waterpaths Saga
The Wolves of Bayou Lune (An ongoing serial on Patreon).

PROLOGUE

*D*ear Tessa,
　　　I just returned from hunting.

I went alone. I'm not yet ready to share that part of myself with Antoine, or anyone else. I'm not sure I even trust myself in those moments when I take human blood. Something happens when I drink that I suspect is beyond what occurs for others. Keziah never said as much, but I saw her looking, sometimes, when I drank. Watching the humans as much as she did me.

Tonight I went inland, away from the river. Through the forest and out onto a small side road. I found a little Mexican bar and grill, a mom-and-pop place with wooden shutters and makeshift tables out front, lanterns hung in the trees. I stayed in the shadows awhile just watching. The people who go there work the land hereabouts for corn or soybeans, on small holdings. I could tell just by looking that the grill is where they come to have a family meal and meet their friends. Children chased one another through the tables, their parents drinking beer from the bottle as they ate the kind of BBQ only Mississippi folks understand. I couldn't look away. It hurt my heart to watch. I thought of you and me when we were small. I thought of the life we used to imagine having, one where we'd get together some place like that and laugh while our own children played with bugs in the dark.

The problem is that as soon as I began thinking those things, the sky clouded over, thunder rumbled, and an uneasy wind scattered the paper plates. It took a moment before I realized the chaos was my fault. And by then, emotion had made me fiercely thirsty.

I took a young man who was on his own. I'd noticed him drinking on the edge of the crowd, quiet and solemn, with lonely eyes and a plain face I'm guessing won him few hearts in high school. He looked like he'd long been resigned to a life alone. After everyone fled indoors to escape the storm made by my broken heart, he lingered to clean up, and I took him as he put discarded bottles into a dumpster by the trees.

He tasted like loneliness and introspection, quiet trees and a river in the stillness of dawn. I saw the clapboard house he grew up in and the infirm father he still cares for. I felt the comfort he finds in small things and the part of himself he'd closed off years earlier, the part that might still have dreamed that his life could be more than isolation and sacrifice.

I reached into that part of him as I drank and felt the barriers there fall away. I felt him surrender to me and his pain flow into my own veins. I welcomed it, Tessa. I want the pain. It doesn't hurt me—it seems to travel through me and become something else. I feel the emotions like waste carried along the great water path inside me. Eventually it disappears, transmuted to become just another part of the rich flow in my body, the particles becoming part of an infinite force inside me. I saw a sharp image of the face he sees when he looks in the mirror, lumpy and misshapen far beyond the reality, and felt his relief as the shame and sadness of that image left him. When I put fangs to my own wrist and held the indigo drops to his mouth, I fed him a new image with his own blood. In place of the misshapen face of his imaginings I gave him instead what I saw: a noble, dignified man who is kind and loving, who cares for his father and works the land left to him—not because he has to, but because he takes a quiet pride in it, and joy in the small gifts life gives him. I gave him the idea that somewhere out there is a girl who will see that man for what he is and love him for it.

When he fell away from my wrist, he was changed. Both softer, and yet somehow clearer, his true self beautiful in the plain lines of his face. He looked at me with eyes free of that dark sadness. He won't be alone much longer, I know. I saw his future companion in my mind: a sweet-faced girl from a nearby town, who will come here one night after her truck breaks down. Theirs will be a true meeting of hearts. I couldn't show him that, but I did plant the surety of it in his heart, and I saw the proof when I looked into his eyes.

Part of me understood this about people before I changed: that if only we could see past the fickle surface covering to the beauty within, we could never be cruel or go to war. That if people could understand their own beauty, they would never be unhappy again. Something about my blood helps people truly know themselves, and part of my gift to them is taking the covering away a little, breaking down the barriers that exist within their hearts. This part of what I am is something I love. Something that makes me feel that drinking from them is an exchange, rather than the selfish, predatory act it seemed before I changed.

Yet for all that understanding, I feel only shame and sadness when I look within myself. I can't look in a mirror. I don't want to. I know my surface covering is dramatically beautiful now. That isn't a boast; it's simply the nature of our kind. We are made to be appealing to humans, designed specifically to draw the prey we need to survive. It's strange how when something is so easily gained, it no longer has value. If I'd imagined myself looking this way when I was still human, I'd have been giddy with excitement. Now beauty has no meaning to me at all. My appearance is just my covering. If anyone could see beneath it to the unworthiness within, they would understand, as I do, that I am not deserving even of life—let alone immortality.

I'm writing this sitting atop a tree. I can see my home in the distance. The sun is coming up, and soon I will have to return and confront the mess I left behind. Antoine tried to talk to me last night, but I couldn't face him. I can't look in his eyes, no matter how much I want to. I'm so ashamed, Tessa. I'm devastated and alone and terrified I will never be able to make right what I have done.

I know, deep inside, that there is no way I can travel the water paths to wherever the twins are now. I want to believe otherwise, and I'm certainly going to try. But one of the gifts given by Katiusca's presence inside me is an instinctive knowing of what is and isn't possible for my form. I can transmute much on this plane, in this time. I sense things that have not yet happened, catch glimpses of coming experiences in the blood of those I drink, though this gift is unreliable and sporadic. I can dematerialize at will and recreate my form instantly in another place. My body is perhaps more alive than that of any other vampire. It can still give life to the earth, exchange it with others. My Indigo, as Keziah called it, is not finite, as Caleb's was. I am a renewable resource, to use modern terminology.

The twins have the Indigo; in the moments before I made them leave, I sensed it in their veins. And I carried them in my own body for nine months. I know them, even if I understand what I know now in a way I didn't when I held their bodies in my own. But I can't travel the twisting water paths into the past. I can't cross time. Neither can most humans. Movement across time is a strange, particular gift. It was the twins who had the power to temporarily transport me along those paths with them. But it takes great effort, and I am not certain of how absolute their power is. It is certainly dangerous. I don't want to say it to anyone, but it is possible Callie is lost somewhere along those misty paths, neither here nor there. It is no place for humans to travel. And no place for babies to be navigating.

I don't know how to bring them all back, Tessa. And I can't live with myself until I do.

I was given two miracles, and I lost them both, along with the girl I love as my own heart. I don't see why any divine being would grant me the miracle of their return.

Your twin,
Harper

CHAPTER 1

CLOUDS

"Surely you have some kind of plan." Jeremiah's voice, tight with tension, is the first I hear as I come slowly up the steps to the back porch. "We've been talking around in circles for days. We can't just sit here and do nothing."

"I'm honestly not sure what we can do, Jeremiah." Antoine's voice is tired and hoarse. I pause just beyond the entrance. I know I should go inside, be part of the conversation, but I can't seem to make my feet move.

"Maybe you don't know what to do. But Guidry does. Shouldn't we be trying to find him?" Jeremiah's voice is hard with anger.

"I've already told you." Antoine's voice has a tight edge of frustration. "Guidry is gone. He left the moment after he knew Harper was safe and Keziah was dead. If he doesn't want to be found, he won't be. I've known him for centuries. Once in wolf form, he can disguise his scent and slip through any net you might cast. He is gone, and we will not find him. You have to let this go, Jeremiah."

"Let it go?" The frustration and pain in Jeremiah's voice makes me wince. "Guidry met her back then. He knew about this all along. That's why he gave Callie that knife and made her memorize the address in Paris. If he knew she was going to go back, why didn't he stop her? And he must know what happens to her in the past. Why won't he tell us?"

These are questions only I can answer. I'm going to have to face them before things get even more ugly between the people I love. I brace myself. I've hidden out here long enough.

"Guidry didn't tell you because he can't."

The group of heads swing around to face me. Antoine looks exhausted. It's as if all the centuries he has lived have carved his face like old wood, grim and hard. He stares at me warily, his eyes opaque, masking his thoughts and emotions. His wariness hurts, though I understand it. Tate looks little better, though gaunt and tired. But it's Jeremiah's eyes that hurt the most. Hard and accusing, they stare at me without a trace of their normal understanding.

"Harper." Jeremiah folds his arms in a gesture so reminiscent of Antoine's that it makes my heart twist. "It's about time."

"Even if Guidry wanted to tell you what he knows, he can't." I ignore Jeremiah's hostility; he's got every right to hate me. "I think that's why he left. He can't tell you about the past because the water paths won't let him. There are some things he can say, others he can't. And I don't believe he knows how to bring Callie back. If he did, he would have found a way to tell us." Antoine, ever practical, is frowning, and I search for the words to explain what I instinctively know. It takes all my self-control to hide my own, tightly held, fury. I might understand what Guidry has done. That doesn't mean I can forgive it. But those emotions are dangerous, likely to result in a tropical storm, or worse. I can't allow myself to feel them. "Guidry waited more than two centuries to be here, at this time," I say carefully. "He's had all that time to try to make sense of whatever facts he has and formulate a plan to help. I don't think even he truly believed it would happen, until now. The water paths back then wouldn't allow him to know what the future held—anymore than they will allow him now to tell you of what occurred in the past." I force myself to meet Jeremiah's eyes. "He lived the past version of these events, but not these ones, not what we do now. If he tries to manipulate them—" I shrug. "I believe he has done all he reasonably can, and that he knows interfering further will possibly endanger us all."

I can't look at Antoine, though I feel his eyes on me like an invisible weight. I know that what I'm saying makes little sense. Antoine's is a mind that takes pleasure in taking apart an engine and reassembling it. What I know cannot be put together in a way he could understand. I can see the twisting pathways in my mind, feel the way they connect and work, but explaining them is like holding mercury. What I know is felt and understood, not unlike breathing was when I was human. I'm aware I'm doing it, but I can't explain the process.

"Water paths," repeats Jeremiah flatly. "What are the water paths? And if there are paths, can't we follow them?"

"Not exactly." I meet Jeremiah's eyes and try not to notice the way he flinches. I remember how it was when Cass first turned, the odd sensation of seeing the girl I'd known blended with someone else and become something entirely new. I know it is the same for Jeremiah— and everyone else—now looking at me. The part of me that is Harper is saddened by that knowledge. Another part of me notices it with detached interest and no emotion at all. "It would be easier if we gathered everyone together and I explained this once, so everyone can understand. Will you call them to come here, so we can talk together?"

"I have to go into town anyway. I'll go and fetch Avery while I'm there." Jeremiah seems only too happy for an excuse to get away.

"I'll fetch Iara and let Connor and Cass know you are back." Tate tries to smile, but it doesn't reach his eyes. I suspect he takes little satisfaction in having been right in his suspicions about Guidry.

A moment later, Antoine and I are alone in the kitchen. Despite the fresh scents of spring outside, the air between us feels still and heavy. Antoine normally leans against the wall, his long legs crossed. Now, though, he stands in the middle of the room with his legs planted firmly hip-width apart, his arms at his sides, fingers deceptively loose. Every inch of his body screams his tension louder than any words could. He is poised for action, like a lethal animal watching a potential threat and assessing the right course of action. His wariness hurts me as much as the pain in his eyes.

I caused this. I'm the reason for his pain.

"Don't be angry at Guidry." It's all I can think of to say. It's an odd thing that despite my own rage at Guidry's actions, I'm still saddened by the rift between Antoine and his oldest friend.

He makes a harsh sound that is closer to a snarl than anything.

"He just wanted to help."

"By sending our children into the past? A strange way to help."

"We'll find a way to get them back, Antoine. I know we will." I know nothing of the kind, and despite all that has changed, it seems Antoine still knows me well enough to know that, because he doesn't answer—he just watches me. "I will find a way," I go on, my voice faltering slightly. "I don't care what I have to do, Antoine. I promise I will find a way to bring them back to you."

He still doesn't answer. I can't read the expression on his face; despite all the extrasensory gifts I have now, I can't read him any more than I ever could. His water path is hidden from me in a way no other is. I can sense the intensity beneath his skin, but I can't feel the pathways inside him as I can with others. I wonder if he is hiding them from me on purpose. The thought hurts.

"You'll bring them back to *me?*" He repeats the words slowly, emphasizing the last. "And then what, Harper? What happens after we get our children back?" He puts the emphasis on the word *our*. I know what he's asking, but I don't know how to answer him. He takes a small step closer to me. I tense, and he halts. I can see a muscle tightening high on his jaw. "What are you planning, Harper?"

"I can't stay." The words come out reluctantly. I know they need to be said, but knowing it doesn't make the dark pain in his eyes any easier to see. I force myself to meet his gaze. "You know I can't, Antoine."

"Don't tell me what I know." His answer comes hard and fast and hits me with a force that makes me sway where I stand. "You don't have any idea what I know, or what these days have been like." His eyes flash gold on cobalt, the hard gleam I've only ever seen when he's facing an enemy.

Which is how he sees me now, I think sadly. I deserve his anger. I must face it. I owe him that much, at least.

"You sent our children into the past and ran away with Keziah. Do you think I don't understand both of those decisions?" He stares at me, waiting for answers I know I can't give. "You sent our children back in time to protect them, and you had no control over Keziah's hold on you. Do you think I don't understand what it feels like, to be under her control, doing things other people don't like to protect them? Have we been living the same life these past two years?"

"It isn't the same."

"Of course it's the same." He's suddenly standing right in front of me, his hands splayed on the wall on either side of my head. "Before you faced Keziah, when you and I met in the kitchen, I told you I would be waiting. Do you remember your reply?"

The Indigo surges through me, leaping toward him, a force of nature that is drawn to him, as the inner part of me always has been.

"Always." The word hangs in the air between us, full of magnolias and sunlight and the promises we thought would be forever.

"I still believe that." Antoine's eyes search mine. "Whatever you think you've become now, Harper, whatever monster you believe yourself to be, I know it isn't true. I know who you are inside. No matter how angry Jeremiah is, or how the others might fear you, I know *you*. And I won't let you push me away." He's so close I can breathe him in, every inch of his familiar skin so close I want only to touch it, to lose myself in it.

No.

A moment later, I'm standing on the lawn behind the house, every part of me alert and unbearably aware. Antoine appears on the porch.

"Don't come any closer." He stops, eyeing me cautiously. "I told you I can't stay, Antoine, and I meant it. It's easier if you understand that." The words rasp painfully in my throat. "I'm immortal, stronger than the oldest of our kind. I will always be in existence. It's just a different kind of *Always* than the one we'd imagined. I can't be here, with you. And you can't ask me to stay. It isn't possible." Despite the clear blue sky and bright spring sun, clouds gather over the river behind me, lightning glimmering behind them. Antoine looks to the clouds and back to me, a slight frown creasing his brow, the storm created by my emotion mirrored in his own eyes. "You see?" I tilt my head back toward the turbulent sky. "That is the least of what happens when I allow emotion to rise to the surface. The power inside me . . . You saw what I did to Keziah. The most powerful vampire of our time, and I ended her with little more than a thought. Can you even begin to imagine how much danger my presence will bring to your life—to the lives of our children? Look at the damage I have already done."

The clouds have thickened and darkened as I've spoken, and now thunder rumbles in the distance.

Antoine doesn't flinch. "How is what you are any different from what I was when I was made? How is the danger you pose to me and our children any greater than that I posed to you and Connor? You didn't run then. You wouldn't let me run. And I won't let you do this. Not to our children. Not to me."

His voice breaks on the last words. He looks away over the trees. When he turns back to me, he has regained his composure, though his tension is palpable in his wide-legged stance, the taut muscle in his jaw. "You don't get to make this decision, Harper. Not after everything we've been through to get to here. We will get our children back first, and then we're going to talk about this. If you run, I will follow you—even if I have to run after you forever. No matter where you go, I will hunt you down and bring you back. I know what you're doing, Harper, and I won't let you. I just won't."

The sound of a truck in the driveway cuts through the charged silence. Antoine whirls away from me and stalks inside.

I stay on the lawn until the clouds over the river have dispersed and the thunder is gone.

CHAPTER 2

RIPPLES

They arrive vehicle by vehicle. I'm reluctant to face anyone until they are all here. After all that Connor and I have faced, I'm reluctant to face him most of all. I'm not certain what I fear more—his reaction to my new form, or his judgement of my actions in sending the twins away. Connor has been my family for most of my life, but the last few years have tested our bond over and again. After all that, the thought of him rejecting me now is unbearably painful.

I remain outside, beside my night garden. It has grown wild in the days since my transformation, strange, violently colored plants I barely recognize springing up all around. In the pond, the two lotuses open in rich folds to the sky, deep indigo, petals dense and strong. I feel a flood of relief. Somewhere, my babies are alive and healthy. I know this, or the lotuses could not be open and alive as they are.

Then I remember that it is sometime, not somewhere. What does it matter if my twins are alive and strong if they are lost in the water paths?

Thunder cracks in the distance, and I force myself to draw a deep, calming breath. I remember Antoine telling me long ago that although vampires technically don't need to breathe, it's a habit that's hard to break. I still find the act of drawing air into my body revitalizing. Perhaps I no longer need oxygen to survive, but I suspect it is just as much a cleansing force as it has ever been, if no longer strictly physically necessary.

I hear Tate and Iara arrive, and I feel Tate coming through the mansion toward me long before he appears at my side and speaks. "I'm glad you've come home, Harper." When I don't answer, he continues, "I hope you will stay."

"I'll stay until I've brought the babies home." I can hear the hard note of defense in my voice.

His smile is gentle. "It would be sad if you found a way to bring them home and then left them to be raised by strangers."

"Antoine is their father, not a stranger. You and Iara are family; Connor and Cass are family. They will be surrounded by people who care for them."

"None of those people can take the place of their mother, Harper." His answer is no less devastating for being delivered in his quiet, courteous tone.

He doesn't flinch when I come close enough to kill him, meeting my eyes with the calm that has always been his dominant characteristic. Now that I see him with heightened perception, I can see Atsila, the medicine woman who was his mother and Antoine's sacrifice, in the lines of his face. It is this, I realize, that lends his face the impression of age. "Do not make this your concern, Tate. I will do what I must."

"And I will say what I must, Harper." There is an uncharacteristic toughness in his voice, a hint of the savage French soldier who had been his own sacrifice. "For three centuries I watched Antoine run alone in the darkness, pushing away everything and everyone who tried to reach him. And then he met you." Tate nods at the mansion behind us. "You made a home for him. Gave him something to care about, enough to want to live, instead of to simply exist. You gave Antoine a life;

and you gave me back my brother, my Maker." Rather than step away from the flashing anger I know is in my eyes, Tate steps closer again. "I won't let you cast him back into that darkness, Harper. I won't watch idly by as Antoine suffers for another three centuries. Whatever you think you must do, you are wrong. What you really must do is bring your children home—and then stay and raise them with the man you married."

Every word hurts. The still water of the pond has begun to move, the surface rippling uneasily despite the tranquil day. Tate looks at it and back at me, frowning. Then his eyes light on the lotuses. "I remember these," he murmurs, kneeling and reaching toward them. "They are linked to your children, Harper, are they not?" His hand touches one of the flowers.

I feel it inside me, an odd, distant tug, like a strange nerve being hit—acutely sensitive but elusive, an unseen pull that makes me look around, startled, then back at Tate. His mouth is open and he seems frozen in place, staring at the lotus. The flower itself is quivering despite the total lack of breeze, vibrating like a tuning fork.

"What was that?" Tate pulls away from the flower and stares at it in fascination. "Was that just me, or did you—"

"I felt it."

He turns to me, and we stare at one another.

"What does it mean?" He looks between the flower and me. "Do you think the flowers are still linked to them somehow?"

"Maybe." I am almost too scared to hope. I kneel beside him and reach out tentatively to touch the petals.

Tate is watching me eagerly. "Can you feel anything? Sense them?"

"No." My heart sinks in disappointment. "Nothing." The lotus stays completely still, not by the slightest quiver responding to my touch. Despite my own resolution to leave as soon as my children are returned, my whole body hurts with what feels like rejection. They already know I'm gone. They've already given up on me.

I'm almost grateful when I hear the others arrive. "I think it's better if we don't mention this for now." I look up to find Tate watching me in concern. I force myself to smile. "I don't want to get their hopes up, Tate."

"But you will think about what happened here?"

"Of course I will. It means something. I just need to work out what." Tate seems to accept my answer, but as we walk back to the house, I can feel his uneasiness. I don't blame him.

I wouldn't trust me either.

Everyone has gathered in the salon. It seems oddly formal, as if what we are discussing is too serious for the cozy, ramshackle kitchen in which I've always felt the most at home. It doesn't help that every face turns to me expectantly when Tate and I appear, every pair of eyes fascinated and wary in equal parts. I can feel Connor's eyes most of all, but I can't bring myself to meet them. Connor is like a wound that leads straight to my heart. I'm just thinking that I'm not quite ready to tear it open yet when I turn and find him staring at me.

In human terms, it is only a brief moment. But to my heightened senses every nuance of emotion, every subtle layer of reaction, is revealed in an instant. And my brother's eyes, though wary, meet mine with nothing but the same unquestioning love and acceptance with which he once assumed sole custody of two small twin girls. I turn away, strengthened by my brother's quiet steadiness.

Cass and Connor are on a chaise by the wall. Avery sits on a dilapidated armchair I'd been planning to restore. Her face, I notice, is hard and closed, and I feel a prickle of unease. I know Avery in this mood; it doesn't bode well. She doesn't quite meet my eyes, and that, too, makes me uneasy. I smile tentatively at Iara, who is seated on a chair by the low coffee table, heart warmed when she smiles affectionately back. Love for her as my Maker spreads through my heart like a soothing balm.

Jeremiah is cross-armed and grim-faced by the door. Antoine stands alone, his arms also folded. They have never seemed more alike to me.

"I thought it might help if Tate and I spoke of what we remember about that time," says Antoine without preamble. "And about those who were a part of it. Between us, our knowledge is not inconsiderable." I notice Jeremiah's face tightening at Antoine's words, but when Antoine shoots him a warning glance, Jeremiah subsides against the wall, his eyes sullen and angry.

"I have been trying to recall all that Guidry ever told me of that time," says Antoine. "And especially anything that he emphasized, perhaps so I might remember it now."

"Ha." Jeremiah's laugh is hard and humorless. "You give him too much credit."

"Lysette is the obvious place to begin." Antoine ignores Jeremiah's interruption. "I've known her on and off for centuries. Not as well as Guidry, of course, but I count her as a friend nonetheless. The last I knew she had a clothing design house in Paris, as you know." He doesn't look at me as he says this. We both know he is referring to the box my wedding dress came in, which had borne the name of her house, Madame Lysette. I can't bear to so much as think of that day, of how happy I was. It seems like another world, one in which I will never live again.

"But in those days, she ran a brothel—a *maison close*, as they were known. She was also the center of the network that Guidry was a part of."

"We know all this," says Jeremiah impatiently.

"Lysette has disappeared." Antoine cuts him off.

Jeremiah's eyes narrow. "What do you mean, she's disappeared?"

"Exactly that." Antoine meets his eyes. "I have a number of

contacts for her. Addresses, phone numbers, email, even social media." He gives a tight smile. "Lysette has always embraced modernity, in every age she has lived. But none of her contact points are giving up any results. In fact, they are shut down altogether. The numbers are cut off, the email addresses invalid, her social media gone. It is as if she has simply vanished into thin air." He shakes his head. "I have the resources to track even the most elusive. If Lysette could be found, I would have found her by now."

"Ramon was close to Lysette." Tate takes up the narrative. "He was heavily involved in her operation, as was his friend, Paolo. But Ramon is dead—and Paolo is suddenly as unavailable as Lysette."

"Why are we having this conversation then?" Jeremiah is visibly furious. "If anyone who might be able to help us is gone or dead?"

"Because they might have left us clues." Antoine keeps his voice even. "If what Harper says is right, about the water paths preventing them from actually talking to us, then perhaps they have tried to tell us things indirectly. We need to try to remember what those things might be." He nods at Tate, who turns to me.

"For example," Tate continues, "there is one name both Antoine and I recall." His eyes linger on me, waiting, I sense, for a reaction, for me to engage in the conversation. But I feel unbearably self-conscious, protective of my being, and, despite the kindness in Connor's eyes, almost frightened of exposing anything of who I am. I feel that if Tate should see me, if any of them could truly see me, that they would run in fear. I am both more powerful than any of them and more dangerous, for I am only barely in control of what I have become. If anyone can see that clearly, it is Tate, who has always been more perceptive than most. My eyes slide away from his.

"During the Regency years," Antoine says, picking up the

narrative and, to my relief, turning attention away from me, "we all spent a lot of time in London. Tate and I recall Lysette and Guidry both mentioning one name in particular: Marie Roux."

"Well, that's a start." Jeremiah is already reaching for his laptop.

"Don't bother." Antoine shakes his head. "Marie is long dead. She wasn't immortal."

"Then what use is she to us?"

"It isn't what use she can be now." Antoine's eyes flicker to me and away again. "It's *what* she was, rather than who. Marie Roux was a witch."

"A witch?" Avery stares at him. "You mean a real, honest-to-god, old-fashioned *witch*?" There is an odd gleam in her eyes. Not for the first time, I wonder where Remy is, and if his absence is the reason for her tension.

"That's exactly what I mean." Antoine's voice doesn't falter. "She was quite famous in certain circles. She was a close associate of Madame Lenormand, the famed Parisian fortune-teller, and was often found in her salon. She was a fierce revolutionary who held the French aristocracy in contempt, but not enough to prevent her taking their money. Tate and I both met her before the Revolution and knew of her during it. But more importantly, Guidry and Lysette mentioned her name enough that it became imprinted upon both our minds. And not just idly, in the way one might mention someone who died a long time ago. They said her name frequently, spoke of how talented she was, how important she had been to their network. Even decades later, long after the French Revolution and the Napoleonic Wars had ended, still Guidry would mention her name. I used to think it was strange, that he remembered her so well; Guidry himself was never much one for the Revolution, you understand. He spent more time rescuing people from it than participating in it. And yet, from everything he said about Marie Roux, she was a passionate revolutionary, born in the backstreets of Paris and fiercely opposed to the aristocracy. I never really understood why Marie Roux held such a prominent place in his memory."

"Wait." All eyes turn to me, and I try not to notice the wariness in their expressions. "I know there was some kind of network in Paris," I say. "But perhaps you better explain a little more about what that was."

Tate glances at Antoine. "There was a—strange kind of understanding between those of us in Paris at that time who had, shall we say, special powers. We did not all know of each other, but those of us who did knew Madame Lysette's as a safe house, a place we could gather or seek shelter as the case might arise. Madame Lysette had a curiosity for all types of supernatural creatures, a compassion for them that tended to overcome our natural mutual suspicion. She took in those who would otherwise have found themselves outcast. Her salon and the nature of those found within it was a secret we would all have gone to our graves to protect, both during the Revolution and later, in Spain, during the Napoleonic Wars."

"Guidry once told me that even though Marie didn't always approve of his rescue missions for members of the aristocracy," Antoine takes up the story, "as a witch, she would still never have betrayed Madam Lysette."

"I still don't understand," says Jeremiah impatiently, "why any of this is important."

"Because I have been thinking over all the things Guidry said over the years." Antoine meets his eyes steadily. "And I think that Marie Roux was there, at Madam Lysette's, on the same night that Callie arrived."

THUNDER

When a crack of thunder splits the calm spring evening, everyone tries not to look at me.

I want to control it. I know I have to learn to keep this power in check. But the thought of my babies out there in the night, lost amid the chaos of war, meeting an unknown witch . . . If I allow myself to dwell on it at all, I feel a savage fury that scares me as much as it disturbs the currents around us. The effect of my emotions on the atmosphere, I know, serves as a reminder to the others in the room of how utterly changed I am, and that in turn makes me feel cold and alone. Antoine is working hard to maintain his emotionless mask. That hurts too —that he must protect me from his own pain, and that I am the cause of it.

Jeremiah is even darker and more furious than I am, if that is possible. "Why do you think this witch was there that night?" In some way, his grim focus is a relief.

Antoine's eyes touch me and slip away. "There is a story Guidry told, many times, about the night he rescued a particular count. The count was to escape on a ship to England. Guidry and his friends chose a night for him to flee when a riot had been planned by the *sans-culottes*, the most passionate revolutionaries, because such nights were always chaos. The man escaped well enough, but Guidry and his friends were very nearly caught by the Garde Nationale. In the melee, he found Marie Roux unconscious on the ground. He knew she would be tortured, or worse, if she was caught, so he took her to Madame Lysette's." Antoine pauses and looks around at us. "Every time Guidry told that story," he says quietly, "he would mention that Lysette had been particularly angry at him. Apparently, Lysette claimed that Guidry had already caused her enough trouble that night—by sending her a young girl, with two newborn babies."

My heart stops. Outside, not a breath of wind disturbs the trees. Inside the parlor, every eye is glued to Antoine. I can sense Jeremiah's rising anger, know he is about to explode in rage that Guidry should know such a thing and run from helping us, but I know, too, the horrid frustration of Guidry's position. I know there is nothing he can offer. And Jeremiah's rage, while I understand it, isn't helping. I force myself to speak.

"What about Lysette?" I hate it when their eyes turn to me, try not to see the fascination and fear in their expressions. "What did she say about that day?"

"We are still trying to recall what, if anything, we might remember." Antoine frowns. "These are conversations which took place two centuries ago, you understand. In the meantime, Tate remembered something else." He nods at Tate, who takes up the story.

"I heard part of the story of that night." Tate frowns. "But not from Lysette. I heard it in London, many years later, from Jeanne, a lady in Lysette's house. She was a maid," he adds hurriedly. "Not a courtesan." He colors faintly, and in other circumstances, it would be amusing to see Tate's impeccable facade ruffled by having to discuss tales of debauchery, but today, I don't care at all. "We were talking together in the kitchen one night about the Revolution, for she had lived those days too. I was speaking of the past—of grief." Iara covers his hand with her own and smiles encouragingly, and I know he means he had been talking of Marguerite. "Perhaps in an effort to comfort me, Jeanne mentioned that she had suffered the loss of her husband. Worse, she said, was the loss of their child. A baby, born during the days of the Terror, who had died of a fever. She said that the one thing that had given her comfort in the aftermath of their deaths was that she had been given two newborn babies to feed and care for."

Something savage clenches inside me. Outside, thunder cracks the sky again. Antoine's eyes, full of concern, scratch at my skin like a toxic plant. I can't stand his concern. I can't bear the pity I feel in the room. My babies have been forced to take refuge in a brothel and feed from a stranger because of what I am, and what I did. I refuse to meet any eyes and just stare at Tate, willing him to go on.

"I did not give it another thought," Tate says, "not until these past few days, when Antoine and I realized where Callie must have gone, and that Lysette has disappeared. I have been trying to recall any detail that may help." He looks at me. "I'm so sorry, Harper. I know this must be upsetting—"

"I'm grateful to her for feeding them." I cut him off, forcing my voice to remain calm. "I hope she did not suffer for it." The thunder recedes, I notice with relief. It seems that the pretense of calm helps to create it. *Interesting.*

Tate's face is agonized. "After the loss of her own baby, I think it was some comfort to her that she could help yours live." I know he is trying to help. It isn't his fault that it just doesn't, at all.

"But this Jeanne isn't alive either, is she." Jeremiah's voice is still flat and hard.

"It's a start, Jeremiah." I can hear the tension in Antoine's voice, and despite Jeremiah's rage, even he must hear the warning in it, because he sullenly subsides.

I look at Tate. "Do you know how long she fed them for? Did she say anything else? Were they—healthy?" Dread grips me. I can't so much as look at Antoine, but I know my own fears are written all over his face. "They were healthy," Tate says hastily. "They must have been. Jeanne would have mentioned it, I'm certain, if not. But it was a conversation in passing, meant as a way to comfort me. I know nothing more, Harper. I'm sorry."

"Damn it!" Jeremiah's fist hits the door frame hard enough to break the skin. "How are we supposed to know anything if everyone who was involved is either dead or has disappeared?"

Despite Tate's restraining hand on Jeremiah's arm, there's nothing in his words that we aren't all thinking.

"There is something more." Despite his even tone and superficially nonchalant posture leaning against the wall, Antoine's unnatural stillness betrays his tension. "Tate and I did some research on Paris during the Revolution. We discovered two things we think might help." He looks at me quickly, then away. "The first is to do with the aristocrat Guidry helped escape that night. I know his name, and it turns out, he wrote an account of his rescue. It gave us a date: the 20th of October, 1793. If there was any doubt, there is also an account of a riot in the area on that night."

"And the second," says Tate, "is that on the 6th of November, two weeks later, La Rose was raided by the Garde Nationale, who suspected it of harboring fugitives—which, of course, it did. Most of the girls were imprisoned. Some were executed. Only a very few escaped."

"But it's April here." Jeremiah looks at me. "When you went back in time, Harper, was it to the same date, just in a different year? Or totally different?"

"I haven't given it any thought before."

Jeremiah looks like he's going to speak, but then he sees my face and subsides. One of the dubious advantages of my transformation, I think ruefully, is the effect I have on others. They're all so terrified of my reactions, they'll do anything to keep me calm. "But now that I think about it, no. There was no date relationship between the time I left and the one in which I arrived," I say, remembering. "Although I did travel to a specific time and place, and return to one, I think it was because Tessa told me how to do so. Which in turn was possibly because the twins had told her how to make that happen. Not to mention that the first time it happened, I came back to the wrong day—to the day before I'd actually left."

"So we have no idea how any of this works at all." Antoine shoots Jeremiah a quelling glance, and he stops talking, though his surly face is comment enough.

"I'm not sure about that." I think back to when I tumbled through time. Now, after my transformation, I understand it differently, can feel the water paths the twins used. "The twins couldn't control it when they were inside me. They fled into the water paths out of fear. The first time, at least, they took me to Tessa because that's who I was thinking of when Keziah appeared. I saw her face in my mind, felt a desire to be in her presence, and that is where we went. The twins may not have understood what I was seeing, but they felt my emotions— comfort, safety, love. They felt where I desired to go. This time, Callie knew where she wanted to go. She had something from that time and the intent to take them all there, so the twins followed her desire, just as they did with me."

"If you planned to get there," Jeremiah says, "how did you manage to come back to the time you did?"

"When I came home, Tessa and I planned it carefully so that I would come back to the point I left. But I think that was necessary because the water paths— they don't really work like time does. Not as we understand it."

I'm grasping for words, unsure how to explain, when Iara interrupts. Her Spanish accent is far more pronounced than I remember, and I feel a stab of guilt at this obvious indication of her exhaustion.

"The water paths are not being one line, with points that are marking different times," she says, drawing one finger across the table to emphasize the linear concept and pointing with the other to indicate stops on it. "They are like the fluid. Water. They are all existing at once, like branches of a river. When we travel them, we are moving from one stream to another, from the flow of one to the movement of another. It is not being this certain thing: *past* and *present*. It is here"—she stands up—"and there." She points to where I am standing across the room. "Path Walkers can move from one to the other. Now they are here." She points to the floor at her feet. "And then they are there." She points again to me.

"Yes." I take up her explanation. "But so long as they are in a particular water path, time moves along that line, as it does in ours. So I think we can assume that as we are living each day here, so they are living each day in their time. Do you agree, Iara?"

"Yes. And no." Iara frowns. "While we do nothing from here, they move from one day to another, as we do. But if we can find a way back to an earlier part of their line, then we will arrive before them."

"Do you think that is possible?" Jeremiah looks between us.

I shake my head slowly. "I don't think so." I try to find the words to explain what I mean. "If we were—Path Walkers, as Iara calls them—perhaps, yes, we could arrive before. But our only link to the past is the twins themselves, and Callie. That means we are linked to the water path through their presence in it. Which means the only way we can go back to where they are is by connecting directly to them."

"And if we're going to do that," Antoine says slowly, "we now have only days to find a way. Because after that, they are gone—and we have no idea to where."

CHAPTER 4

LIGHTNING

It is late afternoon. To my relief, the others have left me in peace, for a while at least. I'm standing in my night garden, staring at the pond and the blue lotuses inside it, when Avery approaches me.

"Avery." I try and fail to force a smile. I notice that she doesn't smile either. I can feel the turbulence of her emotions.

"Two wolves were destroyed in the battle when your children were taken." She says it flatly, without embellishment or emotion. "Did you know that?"

"No." I frown. "I thought the wolves were immortal."

"They're not impervious to vampire venom, Harper. You know this." Her voice is impatient. "It was the newborns who killed them. Their venom, it seems, is faster acting than that of older vampires. That's one of those wolf facts nobody knew until now. Not that anyone has given it much thought. They're all too preoccupied with time travel."

For once, I have no energy for Avery and her constant barbs. I can feel rage just below the surface of my skin, like a prickly heat, dangerous and irritable. "I'm sorry about the wolves, Avery." A sudden wind rips through the trees, and the sky darkens above me. "But I didn't know that. And I don't know how I can help now."

"Nobody does. Remy, though, thinks there are other wolves who might know. Apparently, there are packs up in Kentucky, in the Appalachians. Remy's talking about going to find them."

"I guess that's a good thing, isn't it?" *I don't care,* I think savagely. *I don't care where Remy is going or what anyone does. I won't care about anything again until I know Aurelia and Marguerite are safe.*

"It might be a good thing," says Avery bitterly, "if he was offering to take me with him. Or if he would even make time to talk with me about it. But he hasn't, and he isn't. And I'm pretty sure I'm going to wake up one day to find him just gone." She pauses, as if she's waiting for me to say something, but I feel empty inside. I have nothing to say. I don't have an inch of emotional space left within me. Avery's eyes travel over my face, and finally she steps back, shaking her head. "Here we are again," she says, turning away. "People I care about, dead because they fought for you. Others leaving, also because of you. But you're focused only on what you have lost. I'm sorry about your twins, Harper. I truly am. But you aren't the only person who made sacrifices that night."

She walks away, and the part of me that once would have run after her is angry and turbulent, unable to be what she needs and angry at her for expecting it of me.

The sky roils above, the trees bent with the force of my emotions, and I will myself to calm. I have no time for this. I have to find a way back into the water paths, into time, find a way back to my babies.

I stand by the pond, next to the blue lotuses, and close my eyes. I will myself into the shimmering pathways, trying to find the one in which my babies are alive.

They are alive. I tell myself this every other moment. I know they are, somewhere deep inside. Antoine, I believe, knows it too. But no amount of reassurance makes me feel certain. A terrible, nagging ache gnaws my insides, torturing me with fears I can do nothing to allay except for this: trying to find a way back.

I am stretching every one of my new senses to their limit, and the world around me is reacting. Trees sway though there is no wind. The river beyond has a fierce underwater current that is sending debris spiraling down it with unaccustomed force. The seemingly ever-present thunder rumbles in the distance, purple clouds gathering.

I ignore it all.

I reach within myself, searching through the paths I can feel, probing their depth and shape. The water path that holds my babies is not hidden from me. I simply can't access it, can't slip into it and move. I can feel Aurelia and Marguerite dancing just beyond my reach, maddeningly close.

The sudden awareness that Antoine is nearby makes my eyes fly open. He is standing in front of me, frowning. "What are you doing?"

"I thought that standing in water might make it easier for me to reach them."

His face darkens. "Reach them? You're trying to travel these —*paths*—to find them?"

I don't answer. It doesn't seem necessary.

"Harper." He walks into the pond with complete disregard for the water and grips my arms. His touch sends a subtle ripple through my body, like the current stirring the river beyond. "What happens if you become lost in the water paths yourself?"

"What's the alternative?" I meet his eyes and feel the shock of his nearness, the almost unbearable wanting I have when he is near. A sudden fork of lightning strikes and a crack of thunder splits the air, reminding me exactly why such thoughts are a useless indulgence. I step back from his grasp and his frown deepens. "We have to find a way back to them. They're babies."

My voice cracks on the word. "They don't know how to travel back to us and even if they could, we can't leave Callie there alone. They're lost in the middle of a war, Antoine!"

I turn away abruptly, conscious of the dangerous emotion rising within me. There is a short, charged silence during which I fight to get my emotions under control, feeling the currents around me slowly settling.

Eventually, when the trees have quieted to a soft wave, Antoine asks quietly, "Can you feel them? Do you—sense them, in the paths?"

I'm reminded of the way he has, of somehow knowing where I am within myself. I have not explained anything of what I truly am now, and yet I sense he knows, instinctively, as he always has, what is happening inside me. The thought is both soothing and heartbreaking and I can't let myself dwell on it, or I will lose my composure all over again. And we don't have time for that. Time, I think bitterly, is something I have never truly questioned until now. The greatest irony seems that just as I realize time is something that can be fluid, traveled upon, the linear nature of the world which we actually inhabit has never seemed more constrictive. My twins have access to all the time in the world.

I have none.

"I can sense them, yes." I grope for the words to explain. "But before, when I was human, even though I didn't truly understand what the paths were, I felt—part of them, as if I were walking corridors inside a house. Crossing the paths was like falling through a door, finding myself in another room, though the process was far more chaotic than that. But now . . ." I shake my head. "It's like the paths of time are a house in a photograph, or a movie, rather than a real one. I can see the rooms and the doors leading to them. I can even see— or feel—where in the house the twins are. But I can't enter. I can't open the doors. Their location is as closed to me as a movie would be. Something I can see and feel, but can't be a part of."

The words don't entirely describe how it feels, but they're as close as I can come to explaining. When I look at Antoine, he is watching me with the opaque expression that I know means he has a thought or an idea that he's afraid will upset me. "What?" I step out of the water as he does, trying to follow his eyes. "What are you thinking?"

I feel a pull from behind me that I know is Iara. I am almost as conscious of her presence as I am of Antoine's. It is a different awareness but almost as powerful. I have a similar bond with Iara to what I shared with Tessa or Mom. She is my family, a comfort and a joy, and it brings me happiness when she is close.

"I think Antoine wants to tell you what you already know inside." When she is rested, Iara's English has barely any accent, just a faint lilt that lends her words a certain richness. "You cannot travel the water paths of time, Harper. Not now. Not since your transformation. It is for you now as it was for Antoine before you changed. Our nature is fixed. We are dead, no longer regenerating or governed by water, as humans are. You cannot travel the paths because you are no longer human."

Every word cuts like a knife. Barely ten feet away, a soft rain begins to fall from a cloudless sky.

"But I can move location." My words seem to come from far away. I'm aware of Antoine's concerned eyes watching me, taking in the rain nearby, but I can't look at him. I stare at Iara. "I can travel the paths in a way none of you can, that even Keziah couldn't. I can dematerialize, arrive somewhere else almost instantly, the particles of myself reforming—"

"It is not the same thing, Harper, and you know this."

Her voice is gentle but firm. I turn away from her, my mind moving through what I have known, as she says, somewhere inside. "I can move in this time," I whisper, to myself more than anyone else. "I can travel in the time that is here and now, the time in which I find myself. But I can no longer move along time. I can't . . . bend."

I have a sudden mental image of a tree that has been struck by lightning, burned to a charred, twisted trunk, standing blackened in the fields as the years go by—present, but not alive. "I am dead." My voice is dull and pained. "I am here, but I will never be alive again."

Since the moment of my turning I have not, oddly, thought much on my death. There has been too much life, too much energy, in my new form, for my death to truly seem real. But the image of the tree brings home in a way that nothing else has the knowledge that I am no longer truly of the living. "I can't travel to them," I whisper. "Neither of us can, Antoine."

I'm not certain what I expect them to say. Part of me wants Antoine, at least, to argue. But their pained silence is all the confirmation I need that my words echo his own thoughts.

Through the tumult in my mind, I am vaguely aware of Jeremiah coming down the slope toward us, and with an effort, I slow the rain shower, which has become heavier during my mental process, and then finally make it halt.

"I heard you." Jeremiah starts speaking before he reaches us. "I heard what you just said." He glances at Antoine and then back to me, his face pinched and hard. "You can't travel the water paths because you're a vampire now." He doesn't soften the word, make any effort to ease the impact of it on the still air. "Only humans can move back in time." He moves close to me, too close, and Iara and Antoine both stir uneasily. "It's fine," Jeremiah snaps at them. "Harper won't hurt me. Even if she wants to." He glares at me. "I'm not going to make this easier for you, Harper. If the proximity of my blood makes you uncomfortable, then good. I doubt Callie is very comfortable, trying to survive in an eighteenth-century brothel."

"Jeremiah!" Antoine is suddenly between us. "That isn't fair."

"Isn't it?" Jeremiah's face is stony. "I know your children are there, Antoine. But they can get back. Callie can't." He turns back to me. "Unless you find a way to send me there."

"You?" Antoine frowns. "Even if we could, Jeremiah, how would that help?"

"I'm human, unlike the rest of you. Connor was made using vampire blood, so he can't travel. Even Avery has some kind of special power we don't fully understand. I'm the only one who is truly human. If we can find a way to send me back, then we will also know how to bring Callie and the twins back here. It's the smartest idea, Antoine, and you know it."

"He's right." It's Tate, who has come to stand quietly beside Iara. "If there is a way to send someone back, Jeremiah is the only one of us who can go."

He looks past me into the pond, where the two lotuses are swaying in the water. "If I understand what Iara has told me," Tate says, "those flowers opened the same time the twins were born, did they not, Harper?"

I nod. "That's why I stood here. I hoped that by touching the flowers, I might feel the twins."

"And did you?" Tate is staring at the flowers.

"Yes. But it wasn't the flowers. I can feel the twins with or without them. What I really hoped is that they could help me reach them." *But they can't.* I leave the words unspoken, but the distant rumble in the sky speaks for me.

Tate leans down and touches one of the blue flowers, then pulls back as Cass approaches. I can feel some kind of tension in the air between Tate and Iara at her approach, and suddenly it is too much. Too many people, too much emotion. I need to get away.

And I'm thirsty. I realize with a sickening awareness that I need to feed. It feels wrong, to satisfy my own urges while my twins are lost in time. But Jeremiah's blood is no longer just a vague temptation. It's a roaring lust pounding in my ears.

Cass moves between me and the others. "Harper needs a break." Her voice is not the gentle Cass of old, but the strong, clear woman she has become since her transformation. "Come on," she says to me, already sprinting away. "Let's hunt."

...

Cass and I run into the night.

There is comfort in this, the wildness.

I relax in a way I only have, strangely, with Keziah. Near Antoine I'm terrified of losing control. Near Iara the intimacy is almost unbearable. I love her like a mother, but I am not truly free with her. But with Cass . . . it is exhilarating.

We run far, into another county, and feed on two young men that we find in a roadside bar. They are good, strong country boys, with kind hearts and heavy loads to bear, and we leave them a little lighter.

In the deep of night, we sit atop a high tree in companionable silence. I feel guilty for taking this time but also desperately in need of it. And then Cass speaks.

"I know you're planning to leave."

The tree trembles beneath us. Cass smiles grimly. "I am not afraid of your weather events, Harper, so don't try to hide them." She glances at me. "Don't you think I know how it feels, to want to run? Don't you think I've tried, many times, since I became a vampire?"

I'm surprised into silence.

"Connor has chased me down more times than I can count." Cass looks out over the fields, gleaming silver under the moon. "At first I ran because I was under Keziah's control. Then because I was ashamed of what I was. Then because I hoped Connor could make a life with someone else, a real life. A human life."

I look at her in surprise. "But Connor is a wolf. And he loves you. He became a wolf because of you."

"And that guilt is a burden I will carry for the rest of my existence." Cass's voice is pained. "It's still hard for me to stay, Harper. Especially given that you have something I never will. I would have given anything for children. And now I will never have them."

I'm quiet for a moment, trying to find my words. "But you will take care of mine," I say, the words rasping painfully in my throat. "After I'm gone. They will need you, Cass. And there isn't anyone else I trust as I do you."

"Gone?" Cass leaps to the ground in an elegant move, and I follow her. She glares at me from a short distance, her eyes gleaming red in the night. "You've been granted a gift that none of us—*none*, Harper—can ever have. You have been given miracle children, powers most people couldn't even dream of, and a man who loves you. And still you're talking about leaving?" She steps closer, anger coming off her in waves that beat me like summer heat. "I know all about guilt, Harper. And fear. But they are part of life whether you are a human or a vampire. And neither of them, ever, could justify a mother leaving her children behind." Her mouth twists. "You, of all people, should know how it feels to be alone."

Then she turns and runs, and I am left alone in the night to ponder her words.

CHAPTER 5

LOTUS

In the early hours, I return to my garden and wade into the water, standing knee-deep next to the two blue lotuses. In the still, velvet blackness, they seem to glow with an otherworldly light, like indigo stars as deep and infinite as the universe itself. I don't touch them but just try to feel them, to sense what knowledge may be held in their mysterious folds.

Gradually I become aware of sounds. Voices, snatches of conversation.

Callie's voice, cautious as ever, but curious too.

Have you met others like me before?

An unknown voice responds in French. I understand clearly despite having learned only a little of the language during my human life.

. . . wary of entering such pathways . . . it is easy to become lost . . .

My eyes fly open. The voices fade into the night and no matter how I strain, I cannot retrieve them. *My babies are there!* My preternatural heart thuds in a deep, painful beat. I can *feel* the pathway in which those voices swim. So close it seems all I need do is reach out, and I will touch them. Yet I know they are also deeply, profoundly gone. I stare at the lotuses, which quiver on the water. They are not just a link to the twins, I think, but form a genuine connection with their current reality. And something happened to Tate when he touched them. Perhaps the lotuses are the doorway that opens the path back.

I recall the times I traveled with the twins. I had not thought before of place being significant, for on both occasions that I visited Tessa, I came to her from a different location. But could it help to actually be in Paris, in the place where La Rose once stood? Would it be easier to find them there?

Then that is what I will do. I will go to Paris. I feel better just having some kind of plan. My emotions settle into the calmest they have been since I became what I am. The water around me is still and unruffled.

Day is growing, and I can hear Antoine and Jeremiah's raised voices coming from the kitchen up the slope. I debate for a moment if I should just go now, without seeing anyone, but then consider that perhaps they have discovered something I have not, and so I make my way uphill. I make myself walk at human pace, partly because I am not eager to join them.

The voices float out to greet me long before I reach them.

"Even if I agreed that it was a good idea," Antoine is saying wearily, "I have no idea how we would send you back there, Jeremiah. It is the twins who have the ability to move through the pathways, not us."

"Iara said there are those among the Warao who are Path Walkers." Jeremiah sounds stubborn and angry. "That means someone knows how it can be done. We just need to find them. I'm telling you, Antoine. I *know* I have to do this. I know it." The passion in his voice gives me pause. I sense there is more to what he is saying, and I slip into the room. They turn, startled, and I am reminded yet again how strange my new form is. Antoine is lethal and still in the doorframe, his arms folded, eyes hooded and watchful. I can feel him looking at me, but I avoid his gaze. Every time I see him, I am reminded of all I have lost—and destroyed.

"What do you mean, Jeremiah, that you know you have to do this?"

His eyes are dark, burning caverns in his face, and I am disconcerted at how closely he resembles Antoine. It is not so much his features as the grim, determined expression in his eyes, the taut wariness in his body. "Tell me." I realize with a degree of relief that the air around me is still calm. *I am learning.* I am learning to control it. The thought gives me a tiny grasp on hope.

"I know I'm supposed to find a way back." Jeremiah's voice shakes with intensity. "I *know* it, Harper."

"You've already said that." I am still calm. "I'm asking you why or how you believe that."

"It's like I can see her." Jeremiah frowns. "There. In that time."

"See Callie?"

"Yes, of course Callie!" The burning anger is back. Antoine stiffens and I sense he is about to intervene. I shake my head, a tiny gesture indiscernible to normal eyes, but one his preternatural senses recognize. He subsides.

"I know you're angry, Jeremiah." To my surprise, I'm still calm. "But is it possible that it's your longing for Callie that makes you think you can see her, rather than a genuine vision? I'm not trying to deny your truth." I forestall what I know is about to be a furious response. "I'm just trying to understand it. You and Callie have a strong connection. Perhaps what you see might be able to help us." Jeremiah looks slightly taken aback. "Why don't you tell me what you see?"

Jeremiah is quiet for a moment. The fury in his eyes recedes a little, replaced by the thoughtful introspection that is more familiar to me. He stares at the floorboards. I know he is not seeing the wood grain, but rather into a place beyond this one, where visions drift for us all.

"I keep seeing a wooden table," he says finally. "It's small and round, with low stools on either side of it, and there's a jug in the middle. I can hear voices—women. They're speaking in French."

I feel an odd prickle in my skin.

Antoine moves impatiently, and I know he is about to say that these things are obvious, impressions anyone could imagine. I shoot him a warning glance and he subsides again, but I don't miss the impatient set of his mouth. Oddly, for the first time since all this began, that one familiar quirk lifts my spirits, almost making me smile. It is strangely reassuring to think that even when the world within and around me has gone mad, Antoine's impatience with what he deems fanciful remains a constant. As my heart lifts, a soft breeze stirs the leaves outside, sending a waft of sweet spring air through the open window. Antoine's eyes flare with surprise and fly to me. I keep my own studiously on Jeremiah. "Go on," I urge him. "What else, Jeremiah?"

"They were talking about some kind of plant," says Jeremiah slowly. "But I couldn't hear clearly. It was more—what I felt—"

"What?" I only realize how quickly my question came when they both startle. I consciously soften my voice. "What did you feel, Jeremiah?"

"It's hard to explain." He meets my eyes, and for the first time since I returned, the hostility is absent in his own. "It's like I could smell the room. The scent of old perfume and waste in the streets. And I knew where to go. I knew that around the corner was a knifemaker's shop—"

I freeze. Antoine is also staring at Jeremiah, frowning, as if he too is truly listening for the first time.

"You weren't in the room when Guidry told Callie about that shop," I say slowly. I meet Antoine's eyes. "Did he mention it after I was gone?" But I already know the answer even before Antoine shakes his head slowly, his eyes still on Jeremiah.

"Do you know what the name of that knifemaker is?" I am watching Jeremiah closely.

"Yes." Jeremiah nods, his eyes still slightly unfocused. "It's painted on a wooden sign that hangs over a door. It says *M. Duval, Coutelier*."

My eyes shift to find Antoine's lit with the same hope rising in my chest.

"He couldn't have known that." Antoine's voice is flat, a disguise for the surge of emotion he feels. I nod wordlessly. Jeremiah looks between us both. "Does that mean," he says grimly, "that you finally believe me?"

Antoine's eyes shift back to him, and his mouth twists in the familiar, half smile I have missed so much.

"Yes," he says quietly. "It does, Jeremiah."

CHAPTER 6

WIND

Jeremiah leaves soon after daybreak. "I'm going to find Avery," he tells us tersely. "If anyone understands visions and whispering voices, it's her."

I remember Avery's burning eyes, her hard anger. "I'm not sure she's in any mood to help us."

"She'll help me." There's an edge to Jeremiah's voice. "It isn't me she's angry at."

There was a time I would have responded to the hurt I can feel beneath his words. But that time was before my children were lost to me. Now I simply let him go.

"You're planning something." Antoine waits until Jeremiah is out of earshot before he speaks. We're standing in the salon, by the low round table in the center. I used to always ensure there were fresh flowers upon it. Now old, dead lilies that I vaguely recall cutting in the days before the birth hang limply over the chipped jug I use as a vase, and dust is thick on the table surface. Antoine shifts to stand in front of me, barely a pace separating us. "Won't you tell me what it is, Harper?"

"I'm going to Paris." A slight narrowing of his eyes is the only indication Antoine heard me. That iron control, the rigid discipline—they are aspects of Antoine's character I have heard about, rather than experienced myself. Part of me is sad that I am now one of those against whom he must raise his old defenses.

Another part of me knows that it is better this way. No matter how much it hurts.

"What do you expect to achieve in Paris?" His tone is carefully neutral.

"I can hear snatches of conversation—voices from the past—in the water garden. Vague echoes coming through the pathways. Maybe there, in the same geographical place they are, even if not the same time, I might be able to hear more clearly."

"I'm coming with you."

"You can't, Antoine." His eyes flare with crimson savagery, and I wonder that I so rarely glimpsed that color when I was human. I recall seeing it once or twice, when he was particularly roused by something, but only a brief hint of color, nothing more. Since my transformation, however, I can see the crimson all the time, lurking just behind the deep cobalt and gold. It doesn't scare me. In some ways, it is a comfort to know that Antoine is not entirely the fortress of self-control I had always perceived him to be. That crimson helps me to understand *why* he became that fortress in the first place. And in some odd way, it offers me hope that I, too, may one day be less dangerous to those I love.

But that took him centuries. A cold wind whips through the room, though no windows are open, and the day outside is perfectly pleasant. It twists the dust from the table and blows it across the floor.

"What is it?" Antoine is very still, watching me. "Why can't I come with you?"

I force myself under control with an effort. "You can't move as I can. I will be there in an instant. Even with your speed, it will take you much longer. And we don't have time to waste."

"Harper." Antoine takes a tentative step toward me, as one would to a wild animal. I suppress the savage laugh that chokes my throat at that thought. I know it is slightly hysterical and that if I give voice to it, the wind of earlier is likely to turn into a tornado that takes down the entire salon. I breathe deeply, forcing myself to calm. It all happens in an instant, but Antoine clearly senses it nonetheless, because he halts and watches me with a caution that hurts almost as much as my own thoughts. "Don't you think it would be safer to use what we know we have to work with here? You said you heard them through the flowers in the garden. And Tate said something similar. Now Jeremiah is having visions. That is all happening here, Harper, not in Paris. We know you can't travel to them—"

"We don't *know* that." The words come out before I have a chance to stop them. Antoine nods, and too late, I realize he has seen through me.

"And you think that if you go to Paris, you might find a way back through the pathways that you can't here." He folds his arms and leans against the door frame. "You think that being in the same place they traveled to might remove some kind of barrier, allow you to reach out for them."

"It's possible." I hear the defensive note in my voice.

"Even if it is," Antoine fires back, "what then, Harper? What if you somehow manage to travel back in time? What if you get stuck there, with Callie and our children?"

"I will find a way to send them back. I know I will."

"Them," says Antoine flatly. "You'll find a way to send *them* back. What about you, Harper? What about us?"

I look over his shoulder, into the passage where sunlight falls through the back door, lighting a patch on the old floorboards. As my eyes rest on it, the patch darkens, until a cloud has blocked the sunlight completely. I shift my gaze back to Antoine. "When I look in your eyes now," I say quietly, "I can see the crimson behind them. The savagery that you keep so tightly under control." Antoine's eyes flare in surprise. "I can see, far more clearly than I ever could before, the killer inside you. I was with Keziah, you know. I know what she was. I see her in your eyes."

"Is that it, then?" Antoine's voice is low, resigned. "Now that you see me, see—*her*—you don't want—" his voice cuts off abruptly, and he collects himself with a discipline that breaks something deep inside me. For a moment I consider leaving it like this, letting him believe that is the cause. It would be enough. He would never ask another question of me again.

He would also be broken in a way that no time could ever fix. And no matter what I have become, I do not have it in me to do that.

"No. That's not what I'm saying." I meet his eyes steadily. "It took you centuries to learn to control that part of yourself. I understand that now, better than I ever could have before. I can't even begin to understand how you defied her in those first days, after she turned you. I don't have that kind of control, Antoine." As if to confirm my words, the chill wind gusts through the room again, hollow and fierce. "And our children won't have centuries. They're human, even if they can time travel. They will have decades, at most. We have to get them back. And after we do, I need to let them live their lives in safety. Maybe one day, if I can learn some kind of control, I might be able to know them. To—visit sometimes—" Thunder cracks overhead, and a hard, pounding rain tumbles onto the roof, despite the sunlight I can feel gleaming around the edges of our property. "See?" I gesture helplessly at the roof. "Can you imagine this happening at the school carnival, Antoine? Every time I get tired, or angry, or sad?"

"Why do you assume they will be at a school carnival at all? How do you know they're human?" Antoine is still and, for once, I can't read his eyes.

"Out of all I said, that is what you heard?"

"How?"

I shake my head. "Tate said that Jeanne fed them." I lift a shoulder. "That sounds human enough to me. It isn't like they were asking for blood. And it wasn't some kind of magical pregnancy. They grew exactly like normal babies would. And you said it yourself—my blood made you human. That's how they were conceived in the first place."

"They also carried you back in time. More than once. And then carried Callie back with them when they were barely minutes born." Antoine's rejoinder is swift and decisive. "That is hardly *human*, Harper. The truth is that nobody knows exactly what they are, or how long they have. Not you, not anyone." He steps forward, the earlier caution gone from his eyes. In fact, all his defenses, I realize, are gone. Crimson and gold tumble amid the cobalt, his eyes a shifting sea of the emotions I have always known live within him but have only felt in his touch, in the moments we are truly together. Now I can feel that emotion like a storm in the room, like the weather I make with my own.

"You can't make these decisions alone. I know it seems like you must. It seems easier that way. To shut down, to shut off, until you find a way to live with the darkness inside you. Do you truly think you are alone in that belief? That nobody else has ever felt that way?"

I tremble, and the tumult of rain on the roof lessens slightly, the gloom lightening fractionally. It is so tempting—to reach for him, for the familiar comfort of his embrace, for the reassurance that I won't have to be alone with the storm inside me for long, cold years. "Harper." His eyes glow and he reaches out a hand. "Please. Just trust me. I can help you—"

I don't realize I am backing away until I brush the round table, tipping over the jug. I twist to catch it before it falls, and as I do, my fingers brush the dead flowers hanging from it.

Lightning cracks outside, and I hear Callie's voice, as clear as if she's standing right here. It is sharp with alarm.

I can't recall their names. It's like they are lost to me . . .

"No!"

The vase is upright, the table now between us. The storm outside has taken hold with uncontrolled fury, bending the heavy oaks and casting rain sideways against the mansion, thunder so loud it drowns out almost all sound. "My babies are alone!" I scream over the wind, letting Antoine feel every particle of my fear and hurt. "They're slipping away, I can feel it. And if I don't find them, Antoine, they will be lost forever. I'm going to Paris. I'm going to find a way to reach them, and I *will* bring them back."

"And then what!" Antoine's ferocity matches my own, the storm in his eyes as red and furious as the weather beyond the mansion. "Will you just leave? Because I will never stop searching for you. Never. I will never accept this!" He steps toward me, his hands out. "I love you, Harper, damn it! I love you so much—"

But I won't hear it. I can't hear it. Those words belong to another life, to the girl I was in a small summer church, long ago. Not to the ferocious woman I am become, the furious storm that cannot be tamed, not even by me.

I swirl into the darkness, reaching toward Paris, spinning away from the life I can no longer have.

CHAPTER 7

PARIS

I know where I am going. As the particles of my form begin to take shape, I shift again, so that I materialize on a rooftop overlooking Rue Vivienne, marked by a sign at the end of the street. I am about to drop to the ground below when a vision crosses my mind—the white box in which my wedding dress came.

Maison de Lysette.

It takes me only minutes in an internet café to locate it. Moments after that, I am standing in a quiet alley tucked away in the bustling Faubourg Saint-Honoré fashion district. The Maison de Lysette is a small shop front set into an old stone building. There is a brass nameplate on the red-painted door, which is resolutely shut, and white cloth curtains hang down the interior window, blocking whatever display there may be. The business is clearly closed, even if there is no formal sign announcing the fact.

I pause outside the door, listening closely, but even my senses detect no movement within. The air behind the door feels stale and still. There has been nobody here in some time.

I knew it was a long shot, but I still feel a stab of disappointment, closely followed by one of anger. Madame Lysette is immortal. She facilitated the delivery of my wedding dress. She knew Antoine, Guidry, and Tate in the years after she knew my babies. She *must* know what happened back then. Despite understanding that the water paths prevent certain things, in ways none of us truly understand, anger swells inside me, causing a rush of street litter to swirl in an unexpected gust of wind that startles at least one passerby. A nearby man casts me a curious glance. I catch a glimpse of myself in the glass window of the Maison de Lysette. My hair is a wild tangle that stands out in every direction. I'm barefoot, wearing a summer dress that is entirely unsuited to the chill Paris spring.

I've never cared a whit for the opinion of others, and that hasn't changed. But the last thing I need is unwanted attention, and going by the frowning expressions on two uniforms nearby that look suspiciously like police, I'm about to attract just that. Before they can confront me, I slip into the closest shop door I can see and find myself being stared at with even more disdain by an immaculately dressed shop assistant.

"*Oui?*" she says, not bothering to so much as ask if she can help me. Praying that my abilities of compulsion work regardless of language, I fix her with my eyes. "You will dress me so I look like any other Parisienne woman," I say in a low voice. "You will do it immediately and without drawing any attention, and you will not ask for payment." I make a mental note to come back and compensate her for whatever I take; then, catching a glimpse of the price tags, adjust that to coming back with Antoine's black credit card. That makes me think of all I have left behind, and of the idiocy of even planning such things, and before I know what is happening, a cold gust of wind whips through the store, rippling the dresses and startling the sophisticated clientele.

I get myself under control with an effort. Minutes later, I'm dressed in a simple black wool dress and button-up suede boots, a vivid emerald scarf tied at my neck. I twist my hair into a knot with lightning hands and fix it with a pearl clip, command the shop assistant to forget she ever met me, and slip from the store without being noticed.

A moment later, I am back on Rue Vivienne. Although I no longer look homeless, the stares have not lessened. It's the first time since my change that I've been in a modern city and so visible to others, rather than simply hunting from the shadows. I'm not prepared for the lingering glances cast my way from both women and men. I can feel their interest and emotions; the men are admiring, the women envious. It is uncomfortable. I've never wished more to be invisible, but ironically, I'm more obvious than ever before.

I feel my way along the street. I know when I've reached the place, not because I feel anything, but because the multi-story building is by far the oldest in the street, and if I'd had any doubt, there is an old rose etched into the stone above the doorway. There are also people milling about inside; La Rose, it seems, has become an Italian restaurant in its latest incarnation.

I step inside, nodding and smiling in return to the waiter's greeting, and accept a table in a back corner next to a doorway. As soon as he leaves to get me a glass of wine I have no intention of drinking, I slip out and find myself in a shadowed alcove by a staircase. Through another door to my right, I can hear the bustle of the kitchen, and down the passage to my left, I can see signs for the bathrooms. Sensing footsteps coming closer, I move up the staircase and out of sight.

On the landing I pause. The wall here is painted over with a Mediterranean scene typical of Italian restaurants: terracotta arches framing a cerulean-blue sea, with large urns of olive trees on either side, painted to give the perspective of a distant scene, as if the viewer is sitting on a terrace. But there is something about the painting that gives me the sense it was created to hide something. When I put my hands against it, the space behind the wall feels different—less dense somehow—than the rest of the building. I feel around and almost instantly find what I am looking for: a button in the wall, hidden among the leaves of a painted olive tree. I press it and a crack appears in the painting. I push and the wall swings open, stiffly enough that I suspect it has been many years since it has done so.

I am in an old passageway. Cobwebs hang from the plaster in the corners, and paint peels from the walls. There is an old, threadbare runner on the floor, eaten away in many places. I follow it cautiously until I come to a door on my left. I push it open.

In the middle of the room is a small, round wooden table with low stools on either side. In the middle of the table sits an old pottery jug.

Exactly as Jeremiah described. Something, an eerie, preternatural sense, creeps up my spine. The dust is a thick layer that cannot possibly have been disturbed for decades—if not centuries. *He saw this. Jeremiah really saw this, in his mind.* The still air around me feels heavy, expectant, as if the room has been frozen in time, just waiting for me to arrive.

In the corner is an old porcelain basin. There are no taps; I guess when it was made, there was no indoor plumbing. A small window faces onto a rooftop. It would be unseen from the street, I realize. I push at it and the window opens, but only because of the unusual strength in my arms. It has clearly been long shut. Outside, water has gathered in an old, discarded teacup that is caught between the window and the eaves. On impulse I reach for it. I close the window again and take the teacup over to the basin. Standing in front of it, all I can think of is the sink in the gas station long ago and the answering sink in Tessa's hospital room. *They formed a pathway back then.* Maybe they can now, too.

Closing my eyes, I slowly tip the teacup so the water falls toward my hands.

It happens with the first droplet that touches my skin.

I am caught in a dark indigo chaos that is both terribly familiar and at the same time utterly foreign. I am not tumbling, as I once did. I'm still aware of the room, its vague shape discernible outside the watery, shadowy darkness that shifts around me. Snatches of sound reach me like gusts of wind, taken just as quickly away.

A woman's voice, saying in coarse French: *Do you know what was in them?*

Callie's voice, hoarse with exhaustion and strain: *Nobody does for sure. We think . . . their parent's blood. Before their mother . . .*

The words drift off, tugged away by the darkness.

Another voice, lighter, brisk, impatient: *Well, Marie? Can you do it?*

The first voice again: *I can do only so much, Lysette . . . And perhaps they sense it is not safe . . .*

Dread grips my heart and I want to call that it is safe, that I swear it is safe, when first one sharp, anguished cry cuts the indigo mist, then another, tearing my heart in two. *Aurelia. Marguerite.* I want to scream, to rip through the mist and shadows. I can feel them. They are so close, so unbearably, painfully near—

She is here! The sound of a stool clattering to the floor, a voice filled with fear. It is the first Frenchwoman. *She can hear us.*

Are you here? Callie's voice, strong suddenly, fiercer than I have ever heard her. *If you are here, send me something! Tell us it is safe to send them back. Tell us how to—*

The voice is snatched away and I want to scream in frustration. How am I supposed to send a message through that dense shadow, through the mists of time? They can't hear me, I know it, even if I can them.

Send the wind. From somewhere deep inside comes Tessa's

voice, urgent and clear in the darkness. *Magnolias, Harper. Send them the wind from your garden.*

I draw breath hard into my body, filling it with air. In my mind I fix a picture of the garden at the mansion, feel the red magnolias swaying in the summer winds, the rich scent of them filling my heart and soul. Slowly, steadily, I release the breath, blowing it into the darkness, feeling the scent of my garden meld into the mist, become one with it, get sucked into the indigo and back, into the past.

There is another cry, then a second, this time so heartbreakingly lonely they literally knock me to my knees so I am holding the basin for support. *I am here!* The words pulse from me into the darkness, reaching for my babies, all the love and anguish in my soul calling to them. *Come back to me. I will not rest until I hold you. Come back!*

But already the mists are fading, parting, taking Aurelia and Marguerite's cries with them. I reach out with my mind, trying to grasp the indigo, to bring it back, but all I hear is a faint, desperate whisper that I only just recognize as Callie's.

Tell him, she says, and I can feel the heartbreak even as the words fade with the mist, *tell him I love him.*

"I will!" I shout wildly. This time the words actually echo in the empty room. I am back, the mists are gone, and my voice is uncomfortably loud.

I hear a cry of alarm from the restaurant, the sound of footsteps on the stairs. Without thought, I throw myself through the window just as the door to the small room bursts open, revealing the astonished face of the waiter, as I dematerialize into thin air and am gone.

CHAPTER 8

MISTS

I come to rest in the trees by the mansion. Evening has fallen; I've been away longer than I thought. I had intended to arrive unseen, but Antoine, it seems, has been waiting. I'm no sooner on the ground than he is in front of me, eyes glittering with tension.

"You came back." He says it tightly, but whatever else he was going to say is forestalled by what he sees in my face. "Tell me." His voice is gravelly, hoarse. "Tell me what you found, Harper." There is something in his voice, an echo of my own anguish and loss, that momentarily transcends whatever walls stand between us.

"I heard them, Antoine." My voice breaks on the words. "I heard—" Tears form and begin to fall, and for once there is no matching storm around me, not even rain, just my own grief and fear tumbling down my face. Antoine pulls me roughly against him, and even though I know I shouldn't allow myself this weakness, I can't find the strength to pull away. "They were crying," I whisper brokenly. "Aurelia and Marguerite. They could sense me—and they were crying—"

The rest of my words are lost in tears. Antoine holds me against him, hard enough that I can feel the tears he won't allow himself to shed caught in his chest, a hard lump of pain that I feel as if it were my own. He doesn't speak, just holds me fiercely, and we stand there for a long moment, the world around us temporarily still.

Then I draw a deep breath and the air sighs, the trees beginning to sway again, wind moving restlessly around us. "There's more." I meet his eyes. "I think I know what we can do. But it would be easier if I tell everyone at once."

He nods wordlessly and follows me back to the house without pushing any further. It isn't just me who is exhausted. I can feel Antoine's pain and fear as my own and, oddly, they are a comfort. In this at least, in the longing for our children, we are one.

Jeremiah is waiting for us on the back porch. He opens his mouth to speak, but there must be some kind of warning in Antoine's face, because he subsides, albeit mutinously, and steps aside as I approach. "We'll talk in the salon." Antoine's voice is curt. In a house full of vampires, there's no need for him to repeat himself. A moment later, everyone is gathered in the salon.

"Harper." Connor comes toward me. "Thank God." He embraces me almost as fiercely as Antoine. "I thought you'd gone," he says, his voice muffled against my hair.

"No." I remain in his embrace for a moment. The air moves but doesn't blow with uncontrolled fury, and though I sense electricity in the atmosphere, there is no cracking of thunder. In some strange way, it seems as if the moments I spent in the mists somehow muted my reactions. *Or perhaps,* I think as I pull away from Connor, *it is simply that I have direction now.*

"I went to the place that used to be La Rose." I look around, at Tate's eyes, wary and watchful; at Iara's, full of worry and love. At Cass, perched tensely on the edge of the chaise longue, her hand back in Connor's; and at Avery, sullen and silent against the wall.

Avery.

There is something tickling at the edge of my consciousness, something I can't quite put my finger on.

"It's an Italian restaurant now." I explain about the mural on the wall, the secret passageway, and the room. My gaze falls on Jeremiah, whose eyes burn with the same hollow rage they had when I left. "It was exactly as you described."

He folds his arms and stares back at me. "So?"

"It was *exactly* as you described it." I repeat the words slowly. "Down to the stools and the jug in the middle of the table. They were covered in dust. I don't think they had been disturbed in a very long time." Jeremiah doesn't speak, but he looks a little less angry and a little more engaged as I go on.

I describe what happened in minute detail, including every word that was spoken. I hold nothing back. It's only when I get to the part about the babies crying that my voice falters, and a rumble of thunder comes from beyond the mansion. I feel the reassuring wall of Antoine behind me, the slightest touch of his hand at the base of my spine, and although I know I shouldn't accept this from him, his touch steadies me, as it always has.

"So what does it mean?" Tate is frowning at the floor, trying to puzzle out what I have told them. "What is it that Lysette is asking this woman if she can do?"

"It's the pendants."

I say it with such certainty they all look at me in surprise. "The pendants the babies were wearing—they don't have them."

Antoine steps to my side so I can see his face. "What makes you say that?"

I turn to him. "Think about it. The woman asked if Callie knew what *was* in 'them.' And Callie answered that nobody knows, but that she thought it was Antoine's and my blood. She can't say our names," I say, realizing I haven't explained this. "I think somehow she has lost the power to name us, just as there were things Guidry couldn't tell us. It's part of the magic of the water paths. And I think that is why the pendants are gone. For some reason, they couldn't travel."

"But isn't that exactly what they were made for in the first place?" Jeremiah looks around the room. "To help the twins travel? If they were made for that, why would they not work now?"

"Because I don't think they've been made yet."

My words fall into the room like a heavy stone sinking to the bottom of a pond, slow and weighty, bringing a deathly silence while everyone processes this train of thought.

"You think that is what Lysette was asking the other woman," Tate says slowly. "She was asking if the woman could do it—if she could make the pendants."

I nod. "I think the other woman is that witch you spoke about. The one who you think was there the night the twins arrived. Marie Roux." I turn to Antoine. "We never knew where those pendants came from. It never made any sense for Tessa to have them; I've thought about it a hundred times, wondering how it could be that she didn't know for sure what they were made of. But this makes sense. If they were made back then, by Marie Roux, made to send the twins back here, Tessa wouldn't know. Nobody would, except those who were there, in that time."

Antoine frowns. "But Tessa said she thought they were made with our mingled blood." I'm vaguely aware of the others in the room, but now Antoine and I are talking as if it's just us two. "How is that possible, if we're both here?"

"The vial I gave Callie. Remember? I wore it around my neck. I threw it to her, just before . . ." My voice breaks, but Antoine is nodding, the colors in his eyes shifting with recollection. "I remember. Callie caught it before she disappeared with the twins. So she has our blood with her, the blood you mixed to travel with, back when you were still human?"

Jeremiah's voice breaks the silence in which I am nodding my answer to Antoine. "Nobody knows." His face is ashen. "Not in this time. Not even your sister, who the twins visited often. Nobody knows what the pendants are made of, or how. Don't you understand?" he says bitterly, looking around at us. "If nobody knows how the pendants are made, it means that Callie never makes it back. It means that all the blood is used to get the twins home—but not Callie." He stares accusingly at Antoine and me. "It means she stays there." His voice is bleak and hard. "She makes sure she gets your twins back to you, Harper. But Callie is left behind—all alone, in the middle of the damn French Revolution."

CHAPTER 9

RAIN

Jeremiah brings the gathering to a close by stalking stiffly out of the salon and then out the back door. After a moment, Avery follows him, casting me a resentful look as she goes.

I want to follow him, but I'm guessing I'm the last person either Jeremiah or Avery wants to speak to right now. I wonder wearily why it is that there is always such a price to be paid in order to save what I love. Cass lost her life. My brother became a wolf. Avery has lost Remy, not once, but multiple times.

And now we have all lost Callie. But Jeremiah most of all; Jeremiah has lost Callie.

I think of the final words I heard Callie say, her voice heartbroken and lost: *Tell him . . . tell him I love him.*

It is the only part of the story I left out in my retelling. I know those words were meant for Jeremiah, even if Callie didn't say his name. I want to tell him when we are alone, not with a roomful of people watching. But there is something—an odd shadow lingering in the back of my mind—that makes me hesitate. Something I'm not seeing yet.

"Marie Roux said she could only do *so much.*" Tate is leaning

59

forward, hands clasped between his knees, frowning at the floor. Antoine, arms folded, is leaning against the wall, watching him. "What did she mean by that?"

"She was worried about it being safe, wasn't she?" Cass looks around. "But if Harper sent that—wind—back, and if they sensed her, then surely they must know it's safe?"

But Tate is frowning. "No. I think it's more than that."

"Why?" Antoine asks. It's Iara, though, rather than Tate, who answers.

"I've been telling Tate of the water paths. Of how they work." She meets my eyes, and love rushes through me in a swift, rich wave, comforting and reassuring. "Among my people, it is not unknown for Walkers to become . . . lost in the pathways. It is one of the reasons we do not lightly enter them. To navigate the mists is a skill, one our shamans spend years mastering—lifetimes, even. In my lifetime, Walkers are figures of legend. There has not been even one in my generation; most of our people are thinking that to walk is a lost art, one that is disappearing as the modern world comes closer. And those who might try are afraid of being lost. As the skill of navigation fades, so do those with the wisdom to call the Walkers back."

"Call them back?" Antoine and I speak at the same time.

Iara nods. "But before you ask me how this is done," she says slowly, "I am not knowing. And what I do know, or suspect . . . it would not be possible."

Dread drips heavily through my veins. I already know what it is she doesn't want to say. Part of me has known ever since I stood in that room in Paris.

"It's the blood, isn't it," I say dully. "That is what would form the link, the bridge between where they are now and where we are."

"Blood is what we used, *si*." Iara nods reluctantly.

"But all the blood I mixed when I was human went into that vial. There isn't any left. And my blood now isn't the same. It can't travel. Can it?" I don't need to see Iara's slow-shaking head to know I'm right. Rain begins to fall outside, gray and unrelenting, the clouds low and sullen.

Iara eyes me worriedly. "But perhaps there is another way—"

"No." I spin away from her concern. "There isn't. I know there isn't." I am out of the mansion and down by the river by the time the last word has stopped vibrating in the room. I need fresh air. I need to be away from people. And most of all, I need distance from Antoine. I feel like a hollow eggshell, so empty inside that the slightest touch, particularly from Antoine, will shatter me. I know he will tell me it isn't my fault or try to reach me with compassion, with understanding. I can't bear the thought of it. The only thing holding the carapace of my being together is a thin edge of taut, hard anger—at a world that could take what I love the most from me yet again and hurt so many others in doing so. That anger is all I have to hold on to. It's my lifeline, the only thing that offers some distant hope of a solution. If I allow myself to surrender to Antoine's understanding or Iara's compassion, I will lose my anger—and with it, whatever sanity is left to me.

I'm standing in the shadows of the red magnolia by the river when Jeremiah and Avery's voices become discernible in the darkness. They walk down the slope and onto the jetty, seemingly unaware of my presence.

"I'm so sorry, Jem." I can't remember the last time I heard such a soft note in Avery's voice. It's a reminder that for a long time now, Avery has kept that side of herself apart from me. It shouldn't hurt, but it does.

"Sorry won't bring her back." Jeremiah's voice is as bleak and hard as it had been in the salon. There is a short silence during which I half expect Avery to leave, then Jeremiah lets out an explosive breath, and I see him turn to Avery as he says, "I don't mean to take it out on you, A. I know you're just trying to help." He gives a low cough of hurt laughter. "You know this feeling better than anyone else in there does. Have you heard anything from Remy?"

"No." Avery sits down heavily on the wooden dock, her legs hanging off the edge, and a moment later Jeremiah joins her. I'm motionless in the darkness, wanting to leave what is clearly a private conversation and equally compelled by some unseen instinct to remain where I am. "But that wouldn't bother me so much if I didn't know why he's gone."

"What do you mean, why?" Jeremiah turns to her.

"You don't want to hear this, Jem." Avery touches his shoulder with her own head briefly. "I'm sorry. This is selfish. You have more than enough to worry about."

"At the moment, believe me, it's a welcome diversion." Jeremiah throws a twig into the river with unnecessary force. "If I have to listen to them all talk for one more damned minute about how to get the twins back—" he bites off the rest of his sentence, but not before corrosive guilt crawls through my body. "Anyway. Tell me about Remy."

"Okay. If you're sure?" When Jeremiah just nods, Avery goes on: "What do you know about . . . *mating*?"

"Mating?" I'm as taken aback as Jeremiah sounds. "You mean, like between animals?"

"Yes. Well, kind of." Avery makes an impatient noise. "I'm not explaining this right. It seems that between wolves—wolves like Remy and the pack, at least—mating is more than just a physical thing, or even an emotional one. It's something else. Something more . . . predestined, I guess you could say." When Jeremiah doesn't speak, she goes on. "The night the newborns attacked, two of the wolves died, like I told you. That was hard enough. But a few days after that, a girl showed up at the bayou. A girl from Appalachia—Bailey." Despite all that is happening, I'm caught up in what Avery is saying, unwilling to leave before I understand what is going on. "She was distressed. I mean, like, seriously upset, crying and screaming, asking to see Aiden's body."

"Aiden is one of the wolves who died?" Jeremiah asks.

Avery nods. "He was only just eighteen. Bailey is the same age. And she's a wolf."

"She was Aiden's girlfriend?"

"No. That's just it. She openly said she'd never met him before in her life. Until only recently, she hadn't even known he existed, although she's known since birth that she's a wolf. Her parents are both wolves, and she's been raised in a pack. Then, about two months ago, right about when Aiden himself turned for the first time, she started dreaming about him. Intense dreams. She could see his face, hear him calling to her. The way Bailey tells it, she fought it for all she was worth."

"Fought what?" My own curiosity is mirrored in Jeremiah's voice. But there is more to my staying hidden than curiosity. There's an odd suspicion dawning at the edge of my consciousness that makes me creep closer, listen hard to what Avery is saying.

"Bailey calls it *the Mating*." Avery makes air quotes with her fingers and says the words with exaggerated emphasis. "Bailey said the words like you'd say the Coronation, or the Wedding. Like it's something we should have all known about. Only when she said it, none of us did, not even Remy."

"So what is it, exactly?"

"Apparently, it's what happens between wolves. They don't have girlfriends or partners like the rest of us. Or that is, they might, for a while. But not after the Mating starts. And that's how it usually does start—with dreams, whispers in your sleep. That's how the wolves summon their mates, since more often than not, Bailey says, the Mating happens between packs that are far away from each other. It's like a form of genetic programming that stops the pack from becoming inbred. Once the dreams start, she says the ending is inevitable."

"But none of Remy's pack knew anything about this?" Jeremiah asks.

Avery is silent for a moment, and when she answers, the pain in her voice is undeniable. "As it turns out, some of them did know." She draws her knees up to her chest and rests her chin on them, wrapping her arms tightly around her legs so she is in a protective ball. "Some of them had been dreaming for months," she says quietly. "They hadn't said anything because they all thought it was just a wolf thing, something weird that would go away in time. And some of them already have girlfriends. Wives, even. Turns out, there's only a few among them who *weren't* having those dreams. One of them is Leroy, who recently had a baby girl with his partner."

"The baby they all sensed has the wolf gene?"

Avery nods. "Remy thinks that's why Leroy wasn't having the dreams. Bailey says that sometimes, the wolves partner with humans, most often when they have the gene somewhere dormant in their body. Leroy's partner has Natchez blood, back a ways. We're guessing that's why they're a match. Leroy said the only person he's ever dreamed of is his current partner."

There's a short, pained silence, and I can tell that Jeremiah doesn't want to push Avery for more. Finally, though, he says gently, "Was that why Remy left, A? Was he dreaming of someone?"

"He said he wasn't." Avery swipes her arm across her face, and I realize with a shock that she's crying. "He said he'd never had any of those dreams. But Bailey said something else, and I know it got in his head. She said that the alpha of the pack has to mate with a wolf. That it's one of their 'laws,' whatever that means. That if he doesn't, wolves from her own pack will be down to ask why. She seemed horrified that he would even so much as contemplate being with someone who isn't a wolf." Her voice turns hard with hurt. "Bailey would barely even look at me. She told Remy he has an obligation to take those of his pack who have dreamed of mates up into the mountains, help them make the connections. And she told him it's better if he leaves me now, before the dreams start, and he'll have to leave anyway." Her voice breaks completely.

"Oh, A." Jeremiah's arms go around her, pulling her down onto his shoulder, where she cries in silent, shaking sobs. "I'm so sorry, Avery. I truly am."

I wish I could comfort her, wish I could tell her I'm here. But I'm struck by a thought so dark it makes me still and silent, cold inside.

I listen to Avery cry a while, and then I slip away, suspicion clouding my mind like the storm clouds that roll over the slow-moving river.

CHAPTER 10

I materialize back in my bedroom and stand at the window, looking down the slope to the dock, where the entwined figures of Jeremiah and Avery still sit.

I don't like where my head is going. I don't like it even a bit. And I know there is absolutely no way to prove what I suspect without losing Avery's friendship forever. On the other hand, if I don't ask the question, I ignore the only chance I have of bringing my children home.

Storm clouds roil over the dock, lit from behind with odd lightning. I know those clouds are mine. I'm not even angry about it anymore.

"You will have to speak with her."

I spin around, then relax when I see who it is. Only Iara could manage to get so close without startling me. Her blood is in me; her presence is almost like my own being.

"You know." I look at her curiously. "Or do you just suspect?"

"A little of both, I expect." Shrugging, Iara closes the door behind her and comes closer. "I could feel her tension in the salon. And for a while now, I have thought that Avery has secrets, though I thought they were more about her powers than anything else."

"Her powers?" I frown. "You think Avery is more powerful than she's telling us?"

"Oh, I know this is true." Iara lifts her eyebrows. "I have known this from the start. She has around her many spirits, some of them ancient and very powerful. Her parents, I think, are healers, are they not?"

"They're pharmacists. I guess that is a kind of modern-day healer, yes."

"I think so. Avery has even stronger powers than they do. I think, too, that she knows this, but it frightens her." Iara touches my shoulder. I shiver slightly at the contact; it is thrilling and comforting at once, like a ripple of warmth through my skin. I want to throw myself in her arms as I might once have done with my mother. I want to push her away. I don't know what I want.

"We are lucky," says Iara softly, looking at me with a smile. "I never knew my Maker. Keziah was no more than a voice in my mind. But with you—" She smiles, an expression so full of love it touches my heart. "It is like you are my child," she says wonderingly. "Like I have known you forever. I want to hold you close, keep you safe." Her face twists. "Kill anyone who threatens you." She shrugs slightly, as if a little embarrassed by her own emotion. "I wonder, sometimes, how he could stand it. Antoine. Staying away from Tate all that time. I can't imagine anything more painful than being apart from you for a long time."

"I think it hurt him far more than he will ever say." I recall Antoine's words, long ago, when I asked him about Tate: *I turned Tate because I couldn't stand the thought of living an eternity without him.* But those words were said in confidence, so I don't share them.

"I hope he tells Tate that, one day," says Iara gently.

"You think Tate doesn't already know how much Antoine cares for him?" I frown. "Isn't it obvious?"

"Not, I think, to Tate."

Our conversation is interrupted by a knock on the door. It's Jeremiah; I can feel him. Iara smiles at me. "I will leave you now," she says, going to the window and perching on the ledge. "You will do what is right with your friend, *niña*." A moment later she is gone, dropping silently to the earth and running into the darkness.

I open the door to find Jeremiah looking at me with troubled eyes. "I think we have a problem."

...

"How did you know?" I ask him a while later, after his story has come tumbling out.

"I didn't. Not at first. Not when she told me about the wolves mating. It was only when she said she was going to leave soon that alarm bells started ringing. Then I realized she means to leave now, tonight, and that's when I knew. There's no reason for her to go so suddenly—not unless she has something to hide." He looks at me worriedly. "We have to find her, Harper. Now. Before she leaves."

"I know." I shake my head, staring out the window. "But it would have been so much easier if she had offered. This way, she will never forgive me—or you. Not ever."

"If it helps get Callie back, I don't care." Jeremiah colors but doesn't look away from my raised eyebrows. "Well, I don't," he says defensively.

"There's something else that I heard Callie say, when I was in Paris." Taking in his flushed face and glittering eyes, I know it's time. "Something I didn't want to say in front of the others."

Jeremiah frowns. "What?"

I smile at him. "She knew I was listening. She knew, Jeremiah. And she called out: *Tell him. Tell him I love him.*"

"You don't know that she meant me." His response comes instantly. "It could have been Guidry. She might already have met him, then—"

"It isn't Guidry that Callie loves, Jeremiah." His eyes narrow at the certainty in my tone. "I asked her directly once. She was quite offended that I'd even consider such a thing." My mouth twists at the memory of Callie's face when I'd suggested she might have feelings for Guidry. "The only reason she didn't tell you was because she thought you were settling for her, that she was some kind of second choice. She loves you too much to want that, for either of you. Those words I heard in Paris were meant for you. Of all the things she could have said, of all the messages she could have sent, that was the one she chose. She wants you to know that, Jeremiah, that she loves you. No matter what time she is stuck in, it's you she's thinking of. And if there is one thing I know, it's that love has a magic all its own. If you love one another that much, then there will be a way for you to be together again. I truly believe that. You should believe it, too."

Jeremiah's face is fierce and hurt and hopeful all at once, so full of emotion it hurts my heart. He nods wordlessly, but I know it's because he can't speak, not because he won't. I touch him briefly on the shoulder. "Now I have to go and find Avery," I say gently.

Jeremiah meets my eyes. "Then I'll come with you."

"You don't have to do this, Jeremiah."

He nods slowly and gives me the first real attempt at a smile he has shown since I came back. "Yes, I do," he says quietly. "And Harper? There's something else, before we go." He hesitates for a moment. "I know Callie won't come back." He holds up a hand. "No, don't try to tell me something different. I meant what I said down in the salon. If it was possible for Callie to come back, your twin, Tessa, would have known how those pendants were made. But she didn't, and that means that no matter what happens now, Callie doesn't come back to this time. But that doesn't mean I'm giving up on her." He meets my eyes steadily. "I'm going to find a way to get back to her, Harper. And when I do, I'm going to go to her—and stay there."

I look at him for a long moment, searching through his eyes into the depths of his soul for any hint of doubt, for an indication that he wants me to talk him out of this.

But I don't find any. I don't find even a touch of uncertainty inside him. What I feel instead is the same iron resolve I have often sensed in Antoine, a grim certainty that is not the passionate emotion of a boy, but the quiet knowing of the man Jeremiah was always destined to be.

"Then I will help you, Jeremiah." His eyes flare with surprise. I smile. "I promise you: I will help you in any way I can." We look at each other, for long enough for Jeremiah to know I mean what I say. He nods slowly.

"Then let's go and find Avery," he says. He grins at me crookedly. "Before Antoine works out what's happening. Because once he does, Harper, I guarantee he'll be a whole lot less gentle with her than either of us."

...

I can't dematerialize with Jeremiah, but I can carry him, and despite his obvious distaste at the idea, he's even less happy at the idea of having to explain himself to Antoine if we leave by the front door. So he reluctantly submits, allowing me to pick him up and race through the night to the cabin Avery once shared with Remy on the bayou.

She is hastily shoving things into her hatchback when I alight in the tree shadows just out of her range of vision and put Jeremiah back on his feet. "Woah," he mutters, swaying uncomfortably. "That was super weird, Harper. And if you ever tell anyone you carried me, I will kill you."

"Noted." I force a smile, though my attention is on Avery. "You first?" I breathe in his ear. "Or me?"

Jeremiah turns to me, his eyes dark as the night around us. "Together."

I nod and we step out, the gravel crunching under our feet. Avery swings around, startled, her eyes widening when she sees us. They darken with betrayal as they fix on Jeremiah. "You told her I was leaving," she says accusingly. "I trusted you, Jeremiah."

"He didn't need to tell me." I step forward. "I overheard your conversation on the dock, Avery."

Her eyes grow hard. "That was private."

"I wasn't listening because I wanted to know your secrets. I was listening because of the secret you didn't tell, though I didn't know exactly what it was at the time." I nod at Jeremiah. "Neither of us did."

Avery looks around like a trapped animal. "What secret?" she says, but the hectic color in her cheeks belies her answer, and I know she is just stalling.

"It took me a while to work out why I felt uneasy around you," I say quietly. "At first, I thought it was simply because you're a human, and I crave blood now. But after a while, I realized that wasn't it. Then I thought that maybe it was because you were so angry with me. I didn't blame you for that. I still don't." I take a step closer to her. "But then I realized it was more than that. I realized that what I was feeling from you was guilt, not anger. You weren't angry at me because of what I'd done—or not entirely, at least. You were angry because of what *you'd* done. Because you know that you hold the one thing that I need to get my twins back—and that Jeremiah needs to get Callie back."

"He can't get her back!" Avery flings the words at us as if they are a counterattack. "You said it yourself, Jem! There's no way Callie is coming back. Even if the twins return, she doesn't—"

"And you had *no* right to make that decision for me!" Even I'm taken aback by Jeremiah's roar of fury. Somewhere close by, a dog starts barking, and even the water on the bayou seems to ripple from his anger. "Just as you had no right to keep that blood a secret from Harper—or to take it in the first place."

Avery's shoulders slump, as if hearing the word *blood* sucks all the fight from her body.

"Where is it, Avery?" Jeremiah asks, his voice still hard. "There's no point in hiding it from us, not now."

Sullenly, Avery pulls a backpack from over her shoulder. Rummaging inside it, she comes up with a cylindrical test tube, taken, I'm guessing, from her parent's pharmacy. Inside it, so rich and potent I can almost feel it, is Antoine's and my mixed blood. She looks at me resentfully. "How did you know?"

"It was that day I went to Baton Rouge with Antoine and Iara. The day I traveled back in time and said goodbye to Tessa." I meet her eyes steadily. "You handed me my backpack, said you'd put one of my sweaters inside because it was chilly. Only it wasn't chilly at all that day. And the sweater inside was yours. I remember thinking later that it was odd that you'd done that, but so much was going on that I let it go. It was only tonight, when I heard you talking about Remy and mating, that I realized why you might want some of my blood." Despite myself, I'm curious. "That day was long before you learned about the Mating. How long have you been hoping to turn, Avery?"

"As long as I've known it was possible. Longer, even." Avery's voice breaks, but it is still angry and defiant as she stares at me. "You could have offered," she goes on. "You and Antoine. You could have offered to change me, like you did Connor. After everything I've done to help you, did it never occur to you, even once, to ask if there was anything you could do for me?"

"I didn't offer because I know how dangerous it is." I try not to look at the delicate glass tube in her hand, horribly aware of its fragility. "Avery, you already have supernatural abilities. Powerful ones, too, I understand. Who knows what would happen if you tried to turn yourself into a wolf? Who knows what you might become?"

"Now who's making decisions for other people?" Avery's tone is unforgiving. "And I don't think you have any right to judge what I might *become*, Harper. It isn't me who's planning to leave her own husband and children behind."

Lightning flashes in the night sky, and the bayou cypresses bend with a sudden, vicious gust of wind. I can feel Jeremiah's tension, but he doesn't speak. Avery is still staring at me, an odd triumph in her eyes. "Perhaps," I say, keeping my voice even with a control I didn't know I had, "it's precisely *because* of what I've become that I'm trying to warn you. Whatever you think you want, Avery, please believe me when I say you can't imagine what it might bring you."

"I'm stronger than you, Harper. I always have been. And I know what I want. I've wanted it for a long time." Her eyes shift to Jeremiah. "What about you? When did you work it out?"

"When you said you were leaving tonight." Jeremiah's voice is calm and steady. "There was only one reason to leave in such a hurry. Although I didn't know how you got the blood, or even that you had it, for certain—not until I talked to Harper."

"And now, suddenly, you're on her side. After all she's done to you?" Avery's voice is rising, shrill. Jeremiah stares at her with hard eyes and doesn't answer.

"Avery." I can see the cypresses swaying and know I'm barely seconds away from ripping Avery apart, if that's what it takes to get that blood back into my hands. "What do you want? What can I offer you now to make you give me that blood?"

"I want your help." Her answer comes fast and hard. "Yours and Antoine's. Regardless of what you think I might become. I want your word that you will help me change into a wolf, like you changed Connor. I only need a drop of your blood, Harper —you know that. Hardly anything at all. Just enough to tinge the potion."

I'm shaking my head. "You don't want this. Please. You know what it means. You have to die—"

"Like Connor did. And Cass. And you!" Avery stares at me, her eyes flashing with dark anger. "Do you think I'm not strong enough to do the same for the person I love?"

"No, of course not. But—"

"But nothing!" Avery glares at me, then slowly holds the glass tube out from her body. "Give me your word, Harper, and mean it—or I will throw this blood into the bayou right now. Even if it means you tearing me apart afterwards. Either way, I die."

"I can't make promises on behalf of Antoine."

"Of course you can," she says scornfully. "Antoine will do whatever you ask of him if it means getting the twins back and keeping you. All I'm asking is for a chance at the same love!"

Jeremiah steps forward. "You don't know that's what will happen." His voice is quiet. "You don't know that you're destined to be Remy's mate, Avery. What if he's already dreamed of someone else and just didn't want you to know? What if he's meant to mate with someone else?" He holds out a hand, palm up. "Or—look at Connor. I don't think he ever dreamed of Cass. But they are as together as two people can be. Do you think Connor would leave Cass just because he dreamed of someone else? Do you think it would even be possible for him to love anyone as much as he loves her? How do we really know these dreams are destiny at all, if it comes to that? They may be no more than superstition, a legend handed down among wolves."

"The dreams are real enough that for centuries, people have believed in them." Avery comes right back at him. "Remy wouldn't have lied to me about it. If he'd dreamed of someone else, I know he would have told me. As for Connor— he isn't Natchez. And he isn't me." She raises her hands in a dismissive, impatient gesture. "How will I ever know for sure if I'm meant to be with Remy or not, if I'm not actually a wolf? Anyway— none of this is your business, Jeremiah. It's hers." She turns back to me, her expression defiant. "Change me into a wolf, Harper. That is my price. My condition. Or watch me die now and take the blood with me."

I have been trying to calculate how fast I can get the tube, but Avery is smart. The top is off the tube. Even with vamp speed, I can't catch liquid in thin air, and if it hits the water of the bayou, it will be lost forever.

"Fine." I shake my head, frustrated and sad, but above all, fed up with games. "I can't do this anymore, Avery." Over my head the wind picks up, and she glances around warily, realizing what—or rather who—is making the weather move. "I will help you become a wolf," I say. "But you need to give me that tube. With the lid on it. Right now."

A moment later, the tube is in my hand, lid screwed on tight, and Avery is staring at me with angry, suspicious eyes. "Don't you go back on that promise, Harper," she says as I turn to go. "Don't forget me—or I swear, I will find a way to hurt you."

"I won't forget you." I reach for Jeremiah, but he backs away, muttering that he'll take Avery's car. I rise into the air, already thinking about what comes next.

"Don't forget!" Avery cries after me, but her voice is lost to the wind, and I am tumbling back through space, to the empty rooms of the mansion, and to my husband.

CHAPTER 11

HUNT

When I land back at the mansion, Antoine is standing on the rear porch, waiting. Dawn is close, and the night is still. The lightning and uneasy winds remain behind me, still flashing above the bayou on the Louisiana side of the river, but here the sky is peaceful, the leaves heavy with predawn dew.

"I have the blood we need." I hold up the test tube. "Avery took it."

Antoine's eyes flicker to it, then back to me. "Iara told us." His expression is guarded.

"Antoine." I know I owe him honesty, at least. "I had to make a promise to get it. Avery—"

"Wants me to make her a wolf." Antoine finishes my sentence, his tone almost dismissive. "I should have realized it would come to this, with her."

"I had to promise you would do it, or face losing the blood altogether."

"I don't blame you. It was the right thing to do."

"Then you'll do it?"

"No, Harper. I won't." I'm taken aback by his flat negative.

He meets my eyes squarely. "But we're not going to talk about this now. We don't have time. We have other things we need to discuss—Avery can wait."

Once, I would have argued, but not now. Not while Aurelia and Marguerite are waiting for us. "Do we know what to do? When are we going to get them back?"

"Iara and Tate are working on that. But not today. There are things that need to be organized first." He steps closer. "When was the last time you fed?" I swallow involuntarily. The truth is that dematerializing makes my thirst a savage thing. I've been pushing it aside for hours now, focused first on Paris, then on Avery. But just so much as the mention of feeding is enough to make every nerve in my body spasm in longing. The air around me ripples slightly. Antoine's eyes narrow. "You need to feed," he says bluntly. "We do that first, then we talk." He turns and puts his hand out to me, then glances back, frowning, when I hesitate.

"What is it, Harper?"

I find myself oddly tongue-tied. Hunting with Antoine seems . . . intimate. Revealing. Since I've become what I am, other than a few, recent weak moments, I've kept my distance and myself under tight guard, separate from Antoine. It feels safer that way, for both of us. To reveal my inner being now feels like a tacit agreement that I am ready to begin rebuilding our marriage, forge some kind of future. It seems easier to simply maintain the distance created first by my transformation, then by my time with Keziah. The distance is like a protective barrier behind which I can carefully guard that fierce, uncontrolled part of myself—and ensure the chaotic mess inside me doesn't harm anyone else. In the moments when I feed, however, that barrier falls away, and I'm easily seen for what I am. It was almost bearable to feed with Cass. She's new to this life too, after all, and in her own way, just as self-conscious as I am.

But to feed in front of him feels dangerous. I'm not sure what I'm more afraid of—that he'll truly see me in those moments, or that he'll reject me once he has. Either way, it feels like lifting the lid on my soul's Pandora's box. I don't know if Antoine is ready to see what flies out of it.

I'm no longer the Harper he once knew. I'm wilder inside, dangerous. And strong. I'm not entirely certain Antoine is prepared for any of that. Any more than I myself am.

"Harper." His tone is unbearably gentle. Despite my better judgment, my eyes lift slowly to meet his. In the gray predawn, their deep cobalt shot with warm gold feels like a summer's day, warming some deep recess of my soul I had forgotten existed. "Come with me," he says in a low voice. "Please. Trust me."

I look down at his hand. Taking it feels like a promise I'm not sure I can live up to.

His mouth twists at the edges, and he lowers his hand slowly. "For now," he says quietly, "let's just run together, okay?"

Running. *That I can do.* In fact, I've never wanted to run more in my life.

A moment later he is gone, and a split second after that, I am flying at his side, through the gray river mist and into the wild growth of the forest beyond.

It is exhilarating. Antoine is fast, faster even than Cass, and although I can dematerialize and easily outpace him, there is a joy to be found in running at his side. We leap from treetop to crown, our feet barely skimming the branches, plunging farther into the pine and wire grass until we are deep into wild land, far from the trails and campgrounds frequented by humans. Antoine alights in a clearing as the first rays of sun pierce the morning mist and turns to me, his eyes fiery with the dawn.

"There are loggers working nearby." He tilts his head. "Can you hear them?"

I nod.

"There are two, and they're far from any others. You won't be seen."

But you will see me. I'm too proud to admit I wanted to feed under cover of darkness, to at least have that layer of privacy. Feeding in the raw light of dawn makes me feel even more vulnerable than I do already.

Antoine is watching me. "I can wait here, if you wish." His tone is carefully neutral, his face a controlled mask, and I feel suddenly annoyed that I should still be looking to him to protect me after all this time, after all we've been through and all we have yet to face. I meet his eyes squarely.

"I don't need you to protect me." I'm strangely proud that the wind doesn't blow, that no clouds mar the dawn sky. "You wanted to feed with me," I say, keeping my voice steady with an effort. "Then let's feed."

His mouth curls at the edges. He doesn't answer but just tilts his head, eyebrows lifting slightly, and despite everything, I feel an old, forgotten part of my heart trip. Then I leap into the air, shaking my hair free of its careful Parisienne twist as I go.

I take the younger man as he leans over his truck bed, pulling him silently into the foliage as Antoine takes the other man. I taste the strength and resilience of the logger, his loneliness and determination, his ambition. I see the house he wants and feel the distance between the life he leads and the one he craves, the seeming impossibility of his dreams. I take into myself the hard barriers he has placed between himself and the life he barely dares dream of, and I dissolve them. Then, as I feel the darkness begin to approach, I tear my mouth from his flesh and bite into my own wrist. As I hold it to his mouth, I look up to find Antoine staring at me, and I realize with a shock that he hasn't fed, the man he has taken unconscious in his arms but not yet touched. He has watched me feed. I feel both unbearably exposed and oddly thrilled.

The man I drank from has latched onto my wrist. Knowing

Antoine is watching, I close my eyes briefly, sending the man's dreams back to him with my blood, feeding him the knowledge that they are possible, achievable, and that he is worthy of those dreams.

I lay him gently down to sleep, then raise my eyes again.

Antoine waits until my gaze settles upon him, then slowly, his eyes holding my own, he lowers his mouth to the man's neck.

He takes him with consummate skill, with a sleek elegance that I find almost unbearably erotic. His large hands hold the body to his mouth with casual strength, the corded muscle in his forearms gleaming, and I shiver. I know those hands. I've felt them on every inch of my skin, taking me apart piece by piece, until I am helpless and quivering beneath them.

I watch his mouth work and recall it on my body, relentless and hot on my aching flesh, his hands holding my hips down as I strain against him.

Antoine holds the man effortlessly, his eyes never moving from my own as he takes what he needs, and by the time he pulls away, eyes heavy-lidded and dark, I am trembling with a need fiercer than anything I have ever known. Agonizingly slowly, he raises his own arm to his mouth, then lowers it to feed the other man. I am oblivious to the logger feeding from him. I can see only Antoine's storm-tossed eyes, the slow, rich curve of his mouth as it shifts into the knowing smile I have loved so long. He stretches out his hand to me and, as if I am in a dream, I reach out and take it, feeling the shock of his skin against mine like a summer storm in my veins.

Then he has lowered the body gently to the ground, and we are racing together, hand in hand this time, me following his lead deeper and deeper into the forest, along an invisible path he knows and I do not, until suddenly we are standing in a shaded grove barely twenty yards wide. It is surrounded by great, old laurel oaks, the branches spreading wide and high to tower above us and form an impenetrable wall around, so it feels like our own private sanctuary. The forest floor is covered in kudzu and Japanese climbing fern, soft and thick, and some long-ago-planted wisteria has fought the thick growth to find the sun, wending through the branches so that it hangs, purple and rich, amid the oak. The forest is silent but for our breathing, the grove seeming to have been waiting, just for us.

"I've always wanted to bring you here." Antoine faces me and when he reaches out with his other hand, I take it unthinkingly, lost in the hot depths of his eyes. "Many years ago, when I was a boy, this was where I came to get away from my brothers and father. I used to dream of making a home here, far away from the savagery and corruption into which I'd been born." His thumb strokes gently across my hand, his eyes holding mine, and I have no thought of moving. "I made a camp here, planted things I imagined a wife might like, someday." He half smiles as he nods at the wisteria. "Of course, that was long before any of us knew we shouldn't mess with native forest." His smile fades, his eyes growing darker, his hands pressing gently on mine. "After Keziah, after I became a vampire, I never came back here. This grove was a living embodiment of all I'd lost, all the dreams that would never be mine. More than once, I thought of coming and tearing it down, burning the grove itself, even the whole forest, to the ground. It seemed to symbolize all the life and goodness I had lost. That part of me, I felt, was gone, could never be recaptured. I was irrevocably different. For centuries, I tried—and failed—to accept that." He steps closer, and I can't breathe, can't think, can only be aware of his heat and strength so close. "Until you," he murmurs, his lips so close I can almost feel them on my skin. "Until the day I saw you in the garden at the Marigny mansion and knew, for the first time in three centuries, why I was still in existence."

With one hand he strokes the hair back from my face, and I shiver beneath his touch.

I shiver.

I realize, with a jolt, that the world around me hasn't moved. This shivering is me. My physical body. Not the world around me reacting.

"I never told you this." There is an odd note in his voice that has me listening closely. "I did not see you for the first time in the school parking lot. The first time I saw you, Harper, you were in the garden, digging. You were talking to Connor, telling him about your plans to make a night garden. Your hair was hanging down around your waist." His hand unclasps from my own and twines in my hair, bringing me another step closer. "And when you looked in my direction," he murmurs, his eyes boring into mine, "your eyes were the same color as the emerald ring I'd almost managed to forget. All I could hear was my sister's voice in my mind, the day she gave it back to me." His other hand lets go of mine and slides around my body, drawing me in, and I have no thought of refusing. "Marguerite said: *I hope you live to know, one day, what it is to love as I have.*"

His thumb on the base of my spine is a slow torture, his other hand cradling my head, and all I can do is hear him. "I thought at the time it was a curse," he says quietly. "I thought she meant she wanted me to suffer, as she had, for what I had done. But it was only when I met you that I began to realize what she truly meant. Because even though she was denied a lifetime with Takatoka, Marguerite never regretted loving him, and she never stopped being in love with him. She adored him until the day she died. That was what that ring meant to her. That is why I gave it to you. That emerald meant *always* to Marguerite, meant it from the day she gave herself to Tate until the day she died. This place—" He looks around, at the wisteria hanging in a purple cloud over our heads, at the deep-emerald laurel leaves rich and dark all around. "I haven't come here since the day I buried her. Since I said goodbye to any kind of future that included love." His hands come up to cradle my face, his thumbs stroking my jaw, his eyes as rich and heady as I've ever known them. "It doesn't matter what you think you are now, Harper," he says, his voice barely a hoarse whisper. "There is no darkness within you, no power you possess, that can stop me from loving you. There is no force too fearsome that I cannot love it. And there is no change so great that it could ever alter what I feel for you."

I can feel myself trembling, standing at the edge of a precipice, the fall below vast and terrifying. "I can't control it," I whisper, and this time when I meet his eyes, I allow him to see the wilderness in my soul, the force of nature that runs through me. "I am the wild places and the storm, Antoine. I'm not the girl who stood in that garden, nor the one who married you in that church. I don't know who I am anymore. And if I don't know—" Tears choke my throat, making it hard to bring the words out. "—how can you trust me? How can I trust myself? We have babies, Antoine. Infants who need a mother. And I can't even feed them."

Now the woods begin to stir with my emotions, the trees begin to sway, the wisteria shaking uneasily. Overhead, purple clouds gather swiftly, the now-familiar lighting flashing behind them. "Look." I tilt my head up, his hands still holding my face. "Look at what happens when I so much as *begin* to feel what is inside me, Antoine."

"Look at me, Harper." His voice is strong, commanding, and reluctantly I lower my eyes until they meet his. The cobalt and gold have become something deeper. The crimson is back, and I feel the danger in it like a thick, visceral pulse under my skin. "Look inside me," Antoine says roughly, and I realize with a terrible jolt that I am seeing the man he has kept under fierce guard ever since the day we met. I can feel the heat and rage, the almost-blinding strength, the savage impulses and the intense fear of intimacy. I can feel the years he has walked alone and the iron discipline he has learned—as well as the dark times when the fury within has overwhelmed him. I can taste the blood and regret of those encounters, the anger and self-hatred. With his guard down, his senses are open to me, his heart and soul exposed in a way I know he has never allowed another to see, and it rocks me to my core.

"Don't tell me I don't know the storm." Antoine is, I suddenly realize, only barely hanging on. His voice is rough and his hands on my face tighten, the cords in his forearms standing out with the effort of maintaining his composure. For some reason, his own fight for self-control gives me a courage that I hadn't realized until now I needed.

"If we do this," I whisper, my hands now clutching his face fiercely, "then we do it together, Antoine. It's not going to be easy."

Antoine makes a sound that rumbles up from his chest. "If I'd wanted easy," he growls, "I'd have walked away the first day I saw you."

And then the mouth I have ached for is on mine, the calloused hands tearing the chaste Parisienne dress from my body, and I am ripping the shirt from his. I feel his lips burn on my throat, his hands beneath me lifting me up as I twine around him. I feel the precipice yawning beyond, the danger beckoning me. Antoine groans as he takes me down to the ground with him, and this time, it is the darkness within him that rises to meet my own, and we tumble from the cliff together, into the wild, turbulent places that live within us both.

CHAPTER 12

EL VIAJERO

It is evening again when Antoine and I slowly make our way back to the mansion.

"We should have come back earlier; we don't have time to waste. We need to find our way back through the paths," I say, not for the first time, as we approach the back porch.

"And I told you: after I called him, Tate said he and Iara have some things they are working on first."

"Things like what?" I pause and turn to him, unable to suppress a faint shiver of delight when he touches my arm. I may never become truly accustomed, I think, to how it feels between us now. Amid the grief and terror of our twins' absence, what lies between Antoine and me is a rich, intoxicating gift, one I know I have only begun to rediscover. But for now, all that we are is directed toward regaining Aurelia and Marguerite, and we will not stop until I am holding them both in my arms again. If I lose my own life to do that, then that sacrifice is one I will make without second thought.

"Why don't you ask them yourself?" Antoine nods toward the mansion, where Tate and Iara have appeared on the porch, closely followed by Jeremiah.

"Well?" I look between them. Tate glances at Antoine and me, taking in our disheveled appearance and my hand tucked into Antoine's, and his face softens into a brief smile that nonetheless touches my heart.

"Iara and I have spent the day working through what we know. Matching her knowledge with mine. And Jeremiah has added his own thoughts and research to that." I must look impatient, because Tate smiles again. "I know you want things to happen swiftly, Harper," he says gently. "And I understand that. I do. But we will only get one chance at this. We have to be certain we do it right."

Despite my frustration, I know he's right.

"Well—what can you tell us?"

"There's a lot." Tate exchanges a look with Jeremiah who, I realize, looks utterly shattered with exhaustion. "And as hard as I know it is, I want to ask you to wait until tomorrow, so we can talk properly. There are a few more things Iara and I need to double-check before we tell you what we think we must do."

"If we're right about the timeline," I say tightly, "we've less than two days to do this. I don't see how we have time to double-check—" Antoine presses my hand with his own.

"Tomorrow morning, brother." He eyes Tate grimly. "No later."

Tate nods. Iara presses her cheek briefly to mine, then they are gone. Jeremiah, however, remains on the back porch. "I need to talk to you," he says. "To you both."

...

I go upstairs to shower and change, and an hour or so later, we gather in the kitchen. There is an odd comfort in performing the familiar task of preparing a meal, even if I no longer feel the same way I once did about food. Jeremiah and

Antoine are sitting outside talking, their voices carrying through the window.

"And Tate believes he can open the pathway for you," Antoine is saying. I can hear the detached note to his voice, the shade of disbelief, and clearly so can Jeremiah, because his answer is harsh and direct.

"Tate can tell you about that side of it tomorrow. The part I'm telling you is what you need to understand, Antoine. I'm the only one who can pass through the pathways. I've already seen where I'm going; Harper knows that." He glances back at me, and I nod, ignoring Antoine's slight eye roll.

"One vision is not destiny," Antoine says curtly. "I won't risk your life because of a dream, Jeremiah. And even if Tate and Iara believe they've found a way to send you back, there's no guarantee you could ever return."

"I *want* to go back, Antoine." Jeremiah leans forward. "Even if it means I can't return." I pause, my hands frozen in the act of chopping herbs.

"No." His head shakes once, decisively, then glances over at me. Despite my earlier reassurance that I would help Jeremiah, Antoine's stark negative, his grim-faced tension, highlights the implications of Jeremiah's choice with devastating force. Jeremiah is, I know, the son Antoine has never had. He is family, as much as Tate, myself, or even our daughters.

"Listen." Jeremiah turns his chair so that he is facing both Antoine and me through the window. "Every time Tate touches those flowers in your water garden, Harper, he can feel the pathway inside them. Not just feel it—he can see it." Jeremiah shakes his head. "I'll let him explain it to you tomorrow. But even though he can see it and feel it, he can't *enter* it. Neither can Iara." His eyes fall away from us, slightly guiltily. "They've both tried."

I realize I'm gripping the knife hard enough that my fingers have left imprints in the handle. I don't even want to think about either Iara or Tate being lost in the dark chaos.

"Don't worry." Jeremiah's tone is defensive. "We didn't use the blood. We just wanted to know what we *could* do. Anyway— even though Tate could find the pathway, he couldn't hold a connection to it. That's where he and Iara have gone tonight. To look for something they think can help with that."

"And how do you fit into this?" Antoine is leaning forward, elbows on his knees, hands clasped between them, looking intently at Jeremiah. "Did you also see this pathway?"

"No." Jeremiah's answer is swift and definite. "I can't feel any of the things Tate can or sense them like Iara does. But here's the weird thing." He glances between us. "When Tate and Iara both touched the flowers and then touched me, I was *there*. Inside the pathway. I could see it, Antoine." He's no longer looking at me, but at Antoine alone, his entire face animated. "I could see the room, as if it was at the end of a long, winding tunnel. I knew exactly how it would smell and feel. I could see the rooms beyond it, the layout of the house. I even knew the names of the people I could hear in the distance." He frowns. "The names disappeared as soon as Tate and Iara let go of my hands. It's hard to explain. One moment, I was there, cata-pulting toward that room, and I could feel it calling me, like it was my own life reaching out to pull me in. And the next moment, I was back here, by the water garden, and it felt— wrong, somehow." His forehead creases. "Like this isn't my life anymore. Like I don't really belong here, now. Even the air felt strange on my skin. And one of the names stayed with me, like an echo, or a whisper. The weird thing is that it wasn't even in French."

"No?" Antoine's eyes narrow thoughtfully. He sits back, regarding Jeremiah, his expression slightly unfocused, as if he's gone somewhere within.

Jeremiah looks up at me, then back to Antoine. "I know it sounds crazy," he says quietly. "But I know what I felt."

He rubs a hand over his jaw, which is darkly shadowed with stubble, and on the edge of my peripheral vision, I'm aware that Antoine has tensed. I'm not surprised. Jeremiah looks nothing like the boy I once met at school. His face is gaunt, eyes sunk deep in his face. I realize it has been a long time since Jeremiah slept. He looks so much older than I remember; it hurts, to see him like this. Then my eyes move to Antoine and stop.

He is staring at Jeremiah with an expression of utter shock, completely still, as stunned as an animal caught in headlights.

"What?" Jeremiah frowns at him. "What is it?"

"The name." The words are a hoarse whisper, Antoine's eyes fixed and hollow. "What was the name that stayed with you?" When Jeremiah starts to shake his head in prevarication, Antoine's hand shoots out, grasping Jeremiah's arm in a grip hard enough to make him wince. "Tell me what it was."

Startled, Jeremiah glances at me, then back at Antoine. "It was in Spanish. A—description more than a name, I guess." Antoine's grip tightens. "El Viajero," says Jeremiah hastily, pulling back against Antoine's grasp. "Iara said it means—"

"The traveler." Antoine says it first. "The name means *the traveler.*"

"You've heard it before?"

"I haven't just heard the name." Antoine is as pale as I've ever seen him, colors chasing across his eyes like a storm in the night. "I've met El Viajero." He stares at Jeremiah as if he's seeing him for the first time. "I met him in Spain, in 1812," he says slowly. "That is—I met a man who called himself El Viajero. He never did tell me his real name. And now I know why." He glances at me, then back at Jeremiah. "It's because that man was you, Jeremiah. El Viajero was you."

CHAPTER 13

SPAIN

The silence with which both Jeremiah and I greet this statement is absolute and lasts a long time. It is Jeremiah who finally breaks it.

"You met me," he says flatly. His face has taken on the blank, fixed expression Antoine's does when he is trying to process something internally. "Where? Under what circumstances?" He pauses. "And how can you be sure?"

Antoine stands abruptly and strides across the porch, his face hidden. He reaches down into the bushes and brings up the whiskey he still keeps hidden there. He pours himself a hefty shot, tosses it off, then passes the bottle to Jeremiah. The steaks lie to the side of the grill, forgotten. I don't think any of us have an appetite.

"In 1812," Antoine says, his face still turned away from us, "I was captain of a ship. We were traders on the surface, but in reality, we were reporting to the British forces, under the command of Wellington, and in alliance with the Spaniards, who were fighting against Napoleon. We were not part of the British Navy, you understand." He turns around, facing us both, his eyes far distant. "We reported to a man named Scovell. He was—"

"The codebreaker," breathes Jeremiah, his eyes alight. "George Scovell was the man who broke Napoleon's codes. I've read a book about him. He developed one of the world's first formalized secret services. He ran a ring of spies, known as Guides, who went behind enemy lines."

"Yes, Scovell was all those things." Antoine smiles tightly. "But he didn't do it alone. And much of the information that came to him through his Guides was obtained by others—by those with, shall we say, special skills."

"Like Madame Lysette's network," I say, remembering Guidry's story.

"Yes, that was part of it, certainly. By the time 1812 came around, Madame Lysette was running her house of pleasure in Lisbon instead of Paris. She had set up shop in Portugal in 1806, long enough to establish herself just in time to capitalize on the British forces based there. I recall a friend commenting once that is was almost as if Lysette had known what was coming."

A trickle of premonition rolls up my spine. I come out onto the porch and see Jeremiah watching Antoine intently.

"By 1812, it had been four years since formal war broke out in Spain. The country was in chaos. British ships of the line had the port of Cadíz blockaded, so Napoleon's forces had no way of supplying their southern lines. Guerrilla forces were waging constant battles against Napoleon's armies, and Wellington was beginning to look like he might actually lead the British and Spanish combined forces to a victory. Amid all of this, I landed a party of—special recruits, shall we say—on the southern coast of Spain. We were there to accompany a shipment of rifles from the British forces to the Spanish irregulars, the *guerrilleros*. The comandante to whom we were taking the rifles was particularly unusual, because she was a woman: Lucia Monteleagre. I know I'm telling this the wrong way," Antoine says as Jeremiah shifts impatiently. "I just don't know how else to explain it." He runs a frustrated hand through his hair. I've never known him so discomfited. "To cut a long story short," he goes on, "several of us were captured by a Frenchman of particular savagery, who had an unusual interest in capturing—and torturing—vampires." His mouth tightens. "It looked, for a time, as though not only we, but our entire network, would be exposed." He looks directly at Jeremiah. "Until a man with the code name El Viajero launched a daring plot that set us free.

"Everyone, you must understand, had code names back then. We lived in a world of secrets, where any slip could mean death. El Viajero had been no more to me than a legend, a name whispered in the shadows, a rumor more than a man. It was said that it was El Viajero who was the real mastermind behind both Madame Lysette's network and George Scovell's success. But nobody had ever so much as laid eyes on him. In a world of secrets, that of his identity was the most carefully guarded. His knowledge, people said, was second to none; he seemed to have an almost magical ability to discern where the French forces would be at any given time."

Jeremiah and I are no longer impatient. Both of us are staring at Antoine, waiting on his every word.

"The night that I escaped," Antoine says, "I was taken, with Guidry, to a house in the Spanish city of Granada. Guidry was devastated; the woman he loved, the one I told you about"—he nods at me—"had been lost effecting our escape, though he said nothing to me himself at the time. Guidry and I had gone to the Granada safe house only because I was too badly hurt to be able to travel back to my ship. I didn't know, until I entered the house, that it was the home of El Viajero. Imagine my surprise when the man himself was the first face I saw upon waking. He not only greeted me but asked me to stay with him, share his meals and his home. Guidry was gone—I found out later he had been too blind with grief to face anyone. And Lysette was in

Lisbon. It was just El Viajero and me, for a whole day and night, before I regained strength enough to leave." He meets Jeremiah's eyes, but his own are roaming over Jeremiah's face, searching, it seems, for the face of the man he met that night.

"What—" Jeremiah's voice is hoarse. He clears his throat. "What did we speak of? What—how was my life?"

"I recall it as one of the most pleasant periods I had passed in my long life until that moment." Antoine leans back, pouring himself more whiskey. "We spoke of Mississippi, of my lands here. You said you had been born and raised not far from my own home, but that you had for many years now lived on the continent. You asked me much of my own life, and I found myself telling you more than I customarily did. I asked you many questions, too, but you were elusive in your answers, and I knew better than to press for information you didn't want to give. You would not accept my thanks, I recall. I remember thinking you were one of the most interesting and enigmatic people I had ever met—and by then, after so many years, that was saying a great deal. I asked you, too, what you planned to do when the war was over; you laughed, I remember, and said that there were many wars yet to come. You asked me what I intended to do, and I—angry as I was at that time—said I would no doubt find another of those wars in which to fight. And then you said something I have never forgotten."

"What?" Jeremiah fires the question.

Antoine looks up at him over the whiskey glass, turning it slowly in his hands. "You said you knew that there would come a time when I would cease finding wars; and that when I did, we would meet again." A silence falls after these words, into which the night seems to wait, expectant, for the next part in the story to play out.

"For years," Antoine says slowly, "I thought of those words and wondered what you'd meant. It was many decades before I stopped looking for your face in a crowd, expecting to see it somewhere. Your words stayed with me long after I knew your own life must have ended, for you had told me you were not immortal, nor a supernatural being of any kind. There were those who whispered you were a time traveler, and that was why you took the name El Viajero; but I never knew anyone who truly believed that. I asked Guidry about you more than once, for he spent the majority of the Peninsular Wars in Granada, and I knew he was your close associate. But he would never speak of you, or of anything to do with that time, something I always understood was because of the love he lost during that period."

"And he never told you the name of this love," says Jeremiah, slowly.

"No. He did not."

"When you met me," Jeremiah says stiffly, "was I alone, Antoine?"

"I heard," Antoine says, and I suspect it is only my supernatural perception that hears how carefully he phrases it, "that you had a wife. But I never met her."

"You don't know who she was?"

Antoine shakes his head.

"And you still haven't told me how you are so certain the man you met was me." Jeremiah's face is uncharacteristically grim, his questions direct and hard.

"It was the gesture you made earlier." Antoine mimics raising his hand to his face. "When you rubbed your jaw. I told you that the night I was brought to your house, I was gravely ill. When I woke up, yours was the first face I saw. You were exhausted then, and grief-stricken, too, at the loss of the girl Guidry loved. It was you who told me about her, that she had been lost in the mayhem. But when I woke, you were leaning upon the mantelpiece, staring into the night, and before you knew I was awake, you made that exact same gesture with your hand. I will see it forever in my mind, for the first words I heard when I came back to consciousness were in your voice, bidding me welcome and saying: "I am El Viajero."

...

We talk late into the night. Jeremiah peppers Antoine with question after question, some Antoine can answer, most he cannot. As the night becomes still and deep, the questions finally cease, and then Jeremiah looks at us in turn. "You know what this means," he says flatly. We do, of course, though none of us have said it outright, until this moment. "You know it means I go, and don't come back."

A short silence greets this. Of course that is what Antoine means; but knowing it makes it no easier to acknowledge aloud.

"Perhaps—" I begin, casting about for some unthought of option; but both of them round on me at the same time, with the same word: "*No*."

"There's no time for false hopes, Harper," says Jeremiah when Antoine waves at him to continue. "Antoine has seen what he's seen. That means it happens. It *has* happened. It's done, already part of history. I go back in time, and I stay there. Now all we can do is work out how best to manage my journey into the past—and how we plan to send your babies back to you. With Callie, if it's possible."

"You would send Callie back here?" I frown, exchanging a glance with Antoine. "Knowing you will stay?"

"If she wants to come back, and if I can, then yes, of course I will." Jeremiah's mouth is as set as Antoine's in the same mood, and I know the futility of arguing. "You don't know if it's Callie that I marry. There must be a reason for that. For all I know, it could be Callie who Guidry lost back then."

"I've already told you it's not like that." I shake my head. "Callie said it wasn't, Jeremiah. And I have no sense of anything like that between them."

"But you don't *know*." Jeremiah's words are flat and hard. "The reality is that we barely know anything."

"Let me get something straight." Antoine looks directly at him. "You are determined to do this, to go back in time through the pathways? There is nothing anyone can say that will alter your determination that this is the right thing for you to do?"

Jeremiah nods curtly. "I'm determined to go back. I know it's the right thing to do. I *want* to do it." He looks between us. "And I know I'm not coming back," he says roughly. "I think something inside me has known it from the moment Callie disappeared with that knife. My life is no longer here, with you. It's back there, as this El Viajero, or whatever I am." His eyes move from Antoine to me and back again. "It isn't that I don't care about you," he says, his voice still coarse at the edges. "Because I do. Since you came here, Antoine, all of this—it's the closest I've ever come to having a home, a family. But the truth is that I've never felt like I really belonged. Not here, not anywhere. The only time I've felt at home is with—"

"Callie," I finish softly. "You feel at home with Callie."

He nods. "And even if it means I am stuck in the past forever, without her, I have to go back to where she is. Do you understand what I mean, Antoine? I *have* to go." Antoine holds his eyes for a long time, searching them, trying to find if there is any wavering deep inside that Jeremiah won't acknowledge, I suspect. Finally he sighs, rubbing a hand over his face in a gesture so eerily reminiscent of Jeremiah's own that it gives me chills.

"I know you have to go." He grips Jeremiah's shoulder. "Now, we have to work out how to give you what you need, so you'll be able to stay there."

SUNLIGHT

We part ways at dawn. There are still two days left before our deadline. Jeremiah needs sleep, and weirdly, so do I.

It isn't the physical regeneration of sleep that my body craves, but the mental and emotional relief. With the tact I have long appreciated, Antoine leaves me to sleep and returns to the river house with Jeremiah. I fall into blissful oblivion for several hours. When I wake, the sun is high, the day new, and everything seems possible. Antoine texts to say he and Jeremiah will be over soon. *Can I ask you to wait until we get there before making any decisions?* I text back a simple *yes.* Knowing that Jeremiah is going back makes it slightly easier to accept my own inaction.

Slightly.

Every nerve in my body itches with tension, and if I think for one second about my twins stuck centuries in the past, wind stirs beyond the window and clouds begin to gather. The effect of my emotions agitates me even more, something I'm beginning to understand is a vicious cycle. So instead of indulging it, I look for a distraction.

In the corner of my bedroom lie the rest of the boxes that

Callie and I never got around to unpacking. They're full of clothes, many made by Tessa. They've remained packed away since she died. Mostly because I don't know what else to do, I begin tearing them open.

Every garment has a memory, a day attached to it. But where those memories would once have broken me, now they seem to bring Tessa closer, into the room. The windows are open and a soft breeze ripples the fine stuff of the curtain, carrying with it the scent of river water and the delicate hint of crepe myrtle. I divide the clothes into piles. All those made by Tessa stay, no matter how zany or clumsy they are. Of the rest, most feel like they belong to another life. Packing away the T-shirts and jeans of my old life into a box marked CHARITY feels like saying goodbye to the girl who left Baton Rouge so long ago. I don't quite know yet what will take their place.

I've got all the boxes open and organized in less than an hour. Even taking my time, vamp speed makes the most laborious task pass ridiculously quickly. Halfway through the process, I come across an emerald-green dress made in fuji silk, which feels more like suede than traditional silk. It's not unlike the dress I once wore to marry Antoine, though much less formal. I remember the day Tessa found the fabric, in a little thrift shop in New Orleans. She made the dress for me, but at the time, I couldn't imagine myself wearing it, or attending an occasion where such a rich, sensual dress would be appropriate. Now, though, it seems to fit both my mood and the complexity of my life. It is comforting, too, wearing my sister's memory. I slip it on just as Connor's truck pulls up out front.

I meet him on the porch. "Antoine and Jeremiah are at the river house," I begin.

"I know where they are." Connor doesn't come up the stairs, beckoning me down them instead. "Come with me. I want to talk to you." He leads the way down to the water garden. I find my footsteps slowing as we near it, my eyes uneasily locked on the two indigo lotuses that sit, silent and rich, on the still surface. Odd, iridescent ripples seem to move in their depths like an illusion. *As if they hold the water paths within them.*

"Cass saw Avery last night." Of all the things I was expecting Connor to say, this is perhaps the least likely. I had, if I'm honest, all but forgotten about Avery after all that's happened since I confronted her. Even the mention of her name makes me shift restlessly, and ripples appear on the surface of the water. I'm angry at Avery. And impatient that I must think of her at all.

"I know there are more important things for us to discuss." Connor's hands are on his hips, and he's frowning at the lotuses. "And I understand that all your attention needs to be focused on the twins now, and how you get them back. I want you to know I respect that."

"But?"

He gives me a rueful smile. "It's good to see some things don't change." When I don't smile back, his own fades. "Avery told Cass that she made you promise that Antoine would turn her into a wolf, like he did me."

"I told her that, yes." I look at him briefly. "But Antoine won't do it."

Connor's eyes narrow. "Are you sure?"

"As sure as I can be. Antoine said he won't." I lift a shoulder impatiently. "That means he won't, I guess."

Connor exhales with force. "Okay. Good." He glances sideways at me. "I don't think Avery understands—"

"I honestly don't care, Connor." I cut him off so abruptly he looks taken aback. "I'm sorry," I say, though I'm not, really. "It isn't that I don't care about Avery. But she took the one thing that can bring my children back. She threatened to destroy the only chance we have. I know she thinks I'm self-ish, and that I care only about myself and the people I love." I nod slowly. "And maybe she's right about that." Connor looks at me in surprise. "I *have* always put my own needs before those of others. I married Antoine so you and I could keep this house. I kept the curse a secret from you. I sent my own children back in time." The final words taste like sawdust in my mouth. "I did all those things because, in my heart, at the time, I thought they were the right thing to do." I spin to face him, realizing too late how unnaturally fast the movement is when he takes a startled step back. My hair is rippling in a breeze that isn't there, and I can almost sense the colors shifting across my eyes. As accustomed as Connor is to Cass and Antoine and supernatural in general, part of me knows it is still something else entirely when it is me, his sister, who is the new weird. I know, because I remember how it was for me when he became what he is. "I've agonized over all those choices, Connor. I've questioned again and again whether what I did was selfish or wrong. I've spent countless hours wondering what I could have done differently. If things might have been better, or easier, for those I love, had I made other choices." I laugh. It is a brittle sound, like bark tearing from a tree, and it cuts the air. "Avery isn't the only one who has accused me of acting in my own self-interest. You've said it, more than once. Cass, too. And now here we are again, with people about to not only risk their lives but in Jeremiah's case, change them forever, all to bring my children back." Seeing Connor frown, I gesture impatiently. "I'll explain later. The point is: I know, better than anyone, the consequences my choices have had on those I love. That they're still having." My voice breaks off. I spin back toward the river. "I know better than anyone."

Connor is silent for a while. I'm horribly aware that clouds are roiling overhead, and the air crackles with electricity. I can't help it. I wish I could.

"Is that why you told Cass that you were going to leave?" Connor's question is quiet, but no less devastating.

"She told you."

"Of course she told me." Oddly, I don't hear any recrimination in his tone. "Is that why?" he asks again.

"It's part of the reason, yes."

"And you're still planning to leave?"

I stare out over the wooden dock below us but don't answer. The truth is that after what happened between Antoine and me yesterday, I don't know what I plan to do. All I can think about is getting the twins back. Anything past that belongs to a future that isn't here yet. I know Antoine thinks it is settled between us. And I'd be lying if I said that the refuge of what we are together isn't, for the moment, the greatest comfort I can imagine. But the truth is that I won't know if I can stay or not until my babies are back, and I'm holding them again. If I start to think about being a mother to them, and all the obstacles I face even attempting it, panic rises in me faster than I can control.

"When your mom got sick," Connor says quietly, "I was more or less the same age you are now." His words jolt me out of my own thoughts, take me back to those long ago, gray days, of hushed whispers and bedside pill bottles. "The only parenting I'd experienced was Gareth's drunk chaos and your mom taking me in. I didn't know anything about what a father was supposed to be, let alone how to manage twin girls grieving the loss of their mom. Particularly when one of those twin girls had a medical condition that was life-threatening." His voice is gentle, matter-of-fact rather than tense or bitter, and I find myself listening to every word. "I remember sitting outside your mom's hospital room when you and Tessa were inside saying goodbye. I was surrounded by all this paperwork that I didn't know what to do with. Questions I didn't know how to answer. Terrified they would take you away from me; and even more terrified that if by some miracle I managed to take you home with me, that you'd end up worse off. In all the dark days I'd lived until that moment, I don't think I'd ever felt so utterly inadequate to a task in my life as I did becoming your sole caregiver."

"But you'd already been caring for us." I'm temporarily shocked out of my current reality. "You'd been a parent to Tessa and me for more than a year by then. It never even occurred to us that we wouldn't be going home with you that day."

"Well, believe me—it wasn't simple. And it very nearly didn't happen." When I turn to him, startled, Connor nods slowly, holding my eyes. "There were doctors and social workers and everything in between. They all had an opinion, a thousand dire warnings, and a mountain of paperwork I had no idea how to complete. Not that I needed any help with being afraid. I was already convinced that I was the last person who should be raising you." His mouth twists in a pained smile. "I started to walk out of that hospital a half dozen times that night. Twice, I got so far as that damn fountain out front. I knew I didn't have the strength to say goodbye to you. But I thought that if I just left—let the experts take control and do my explaining for me— that you'd be better off. I couldn't for the life of me imagine any scenario where my staying would be the right thing."

"Then why did you?" My voice is thin, barely there.

"Because no matter how terrible Gareth was as a father, I still would have done anything for him to stay. Anything." There is such bleakness in his tone my heart clenches. "I figured that the only thing worse than having me for a parent figure would be having nobody at all. And I guess that I knew, deep down, that I might be able to live with making a thousand mistakes— but I could never live with the knowledge that I'd left you alone when you needed me most.

"But that feeling never went away, Harper. Every time I dealt with a teacher or a doctor or Social Services, every time I caught a sneering look from another parent—or, even worse, the judgmental, suspicious looks when people assumed there was something inappropriate in our relationship—every one of those moments left me wracked with insecurity and self-doubt. Right up to, I might add, the discovery that you had not only concealed a curse in our cellar from me, but you married a vampire to keep it a secret." He arches his eyebrows in a sardonic look that almost makes me smile. "If you think you have doubts about your parenting skills, Harper, can you imagine how I felt about mine that day? All I could think was that I'd failed you. Utterly failed you. That if I had just left parenting to the experts, hadn't tried to make some stupid family fantasy come true, you'd have had a chance at a normal life."

"But that's not true at all!" I'm shocked out of silence. "You were—everything, Connor. To Tessa and to me. And despite everything that's happened, you still are. This weird life we have now, it's still a family. And I still need you. My children are going to need you—" I choke on the last words, and the silence that falls is alive with the meaning behind them.

"You mean," Connor says finally, "that your twins are going to need me and Cass, because you won't be here to raise them. Don't you, Harper?"

"I can't." My voice breaks completely, and all around us, rain begins to fall in a soft, gray curtain. "I can't raise them. Look at everything I have broken. All that my decisions have cost, even still. Callie." My voice falters, but I force myself to continue. "She's lost, Connor. Gone. Your only blood sister, and she might very well be lost to us forever."

"And if Callie were here, she would make the same choice again. In a heartbeat. I know she would. I don't blame you for that, Harper. None of us do. And although I wish Callie was here, and that we had more time together, I believe that wherever she is, she will find a way to be happy." He smiles crookedly. "It's the way that girl is built. Tough. It might be the only thing Gareth gave us both—the will to survive, no matter what life throws at us."

"But after all I've done," I say, my voice barely a whisper, "how will I ever know that I am making the right decisions for the twins? How can I possibly trust myself to do the right thing? I can't even control the damned *weather*—"

And then I am truly crying, all the inner, terrified parts of my soul pouring down my cheeks and all around us in an unstoppable torrent, and my brother's arms are around me, the comforting wall they have been for so long. And I dare to imagine, for one cold, terrifying moment, what these years would have been like if I had never had Connor to share them with. "I couldn't have survived all this," I say thickly against his chest. "I couldn't have done any of it without you. You might think you made mistakes. But all I ever saw when I looked at you was home. You *were* my home, Connor. You still are."

"And that is exactly what you are to your twins," he murmurs against my hair. "I know you don't believe it. I know you can't imagine for a second how you're going to do this. But I promise: you will find a way. And you'll make mistakes, and your girls will shout and argue, and people will judge you—whether they're vampires, wolves, or humans. It's going to be messy and unpredictable, and there are going to be no certain outcomes." He pulls away and holds my shoulders, staring into my eyes. "But if you leave, Harper," he says softly, "there will be only one outcome: your girls will have lost their mother. Not because she died or because they were taken away, but because she *chose* to leave them. And it won't matter how much other people love them or what reasons you give them when you're older; you will never be able to take that outcome away. I don't think you want that, Harper. And I don't want it for you."

I shake my head. I try to speak, but the words come out a hoarse whisper. "I don't want that either." I draw a ragged breath and above, a shaft of sunlight pierces the gray veil of rain. I meet his eyes, and when I see the question in them, I nod silently. He pulls me against him. We stand there for a long moment, in the still cocoon of my tears. And of all the promises

I have made, this one, I know, is the most profound, even if it is unspoken.

I hear Antoine's truck coming up the road, and Connor pulls back from me, smiling crookedly. "Now clear those rainclouds," he says, wiping his thumbs under my eyes, "before your husband decides they're my fault. And let's work out how we're going to bring my nieces home. Okay?"

I nod. "Okay," I whisper, slipping my hand into his and giving him a watery smile. "Okay."

CHAPTER 15

Connor halts just outside the mansion and turns to me, his hands gentle on my shoulders. "Are you going to be okay?"

"You're not staying?"

"I'm only a phone call away. As soon as you need us, just text. But it's only Jeremiah and Antoine in there. I think they might want to talk without me in the way." He smiles and hugs me briefly and is gone.

I take a deep breath, compose myself, and go inside.

Jeremiah and Antoine are waiting for me in the salon. "Tate will be here soon," Antoine says by way of greeting. "I asked him to give us an hour or so."

"What did you find out?" I perch on the chaise longue, looking between them. Jeremiah is in a large leather chair I'd been planning to re-cover, before all this started. Antoine is leaning against the door frame. He eyes me, taking in the traces of tears, but he doesn't ask me questions, and for that I'm grateful.

"A few things worth taking note of." Antoine holds out a

piece of paper. It's old and faded, with French writing in a spidery hand.

"What is this?" I look up from it. "My French isn't good enough to understand."

"It's a letter I received from my Paris creditors in 1794, advising me that a substantial sum had been withdrawn in gold from my account, according to a draft presented by a Lysette Baudelaire."

"Madame Lysette?"

Antoine nods. "I was in England at the time, and the letter didn't reach me until long after the draft had been presented. By that time, Lysette had sent Guidry to ask if I would contribute to the network she had set up in France. I didn't hesitate to give him a letter of authorization to take whatever he needed. I, too, had friends and family caught up in the Terror. It never occurred to me to check the date that the draft was presented; I just assumed the sum was withdrawn after I issued the authorization. Until now, that is. I was trying to remember if I'd had any odd requests for money at that time, and the one from Lysette was all I could think of. I spent most of the night looking through my records of that time until I found it. When I did, I saw this." He points to the date written at the top of the page.

"The 5th of November," I breathe. I look up at them both. "The day before the raid on La Rose."

"And a good month or more before I signed the letter of authorization. Which wouldn't have been needed," Antoine adds, "if the drawer arrived at the bank holding a draft with my signature."

"But this sum," I say, scrutinizing the strange writing, "it's a lot?"

"It's a fortune," Jeremiah says bluntly. "Enough to buy an entire estate in England at the time."

"Or fund a spy network," says Antoine dryly. "Which I thought I was doing."

"And you think this money was for Jeremiah?"

"I'm sure of it. There's no way the bank would have issued this kind of sum without a written draft from me. And I wouldn't have noticed it was gone. I didn't care much for coin back then." Antoine shrugs. "I had more than I would ever spend already. Besides, France was in chaos. Nobody knew what would happen there. I was focused on my holdings in England and India, where trade was booming. I still had a house in Paris, but whatever liquid assets were left in my bank in Paris I had already written off as a loss. And by the time this letter reached me, I was already at sea, my attention focused on the brewing tension in the channel and along the French coast. Apart from a cursory opening of the envelope to check the contents, I wouldn't have given it a second thought."

"So this draft—you're going to write it here?"

Jeremiah grins. "This is where being a vampire and having a history nerd in the house comes in handy." I realize, with a slight shock, that Jeremiah is the most animated I've ever seen him. It's as if having a purpose has galvanized him, put hope back where there was only darkness. "Antoine still has some of his old letterheads from that time. They're a bit aged, but nothing that would raise suspicion."

"You kept old letterheads?" I look at Antoine quizzically

"Believe me, not from sentiment," says Antoine hastily. "But if immortality teaches anything, it's the value of original documents. One never knows when a forgery may be required."

I shake my head, amused despite myself. "You have a criminal turn of mind, both of you. Do you know that?"

Jeremiah grins and holds up a rolled document, sealed with wax and tied with cord. "*Et voilà.* One bank draft, made out to Lysette Baudelaire." He holds up a second. "And another, made out to Jeremiah Marigny. Just in case."

"Why two?" I look between them, frowning. "Why can't Jeremiah just use his own?"

"Well, that's the bad news, I guess." Antoine nods at Jeremiah, who shifts restlessly in his chair.

"The thing is," Jeremiah says, eyeing me cautiously, "while there is a clear account of Lysette Baudelaire taking money from the account, there's no record of a Jeremiah Marigny. Not in Antoine's bank documents, not in the family history. Not anywhere. It's as if I never exist in that time at all." I can feel their mutual tension, all the questions they're expecting from me, but every time I start to give them voice, I realize the impossibility of receiving an answer. Nobody knows the answers. We can't. None of it has actually happened yet. Or it has, but . . . I shake my head impatiently. It's too hard to keep track of.

"What about Callie's name?" I know it's probably a futile question, but I have to ask it. I feel an odd shiver in the air and turn to Antoine, but he has his back to me, leaning over something on the floor, so I can't see his face.

"We can't find anything there either." Jeremiah holds up another sealed document. "But we've got a bank draft in her name, too. Just in case."

"What else have you got?" I'm starting to feel like I've missed an entire chapter of a story.

Antoine turns back to us, holding up a leather bag, and I realize it must have been the bag itself that impacted the atmosphere in the room. Though the leather is well-kept, it is clearly very old, and it has initials on the side: AJM. *Antoine Jacques Marigny.* A bag from the past.

"Era-appropriate clothes, toiletries, and accessories," Antoine says, holding up a hand and counting off on his fingers. "Identity papers, though there are others that will need to be made there, according to circumstances. Lysette can help with that, I am certain. Letters of recommendation to every salon and establishment worthy of note in Paris at the time. All with the name left blank—"

"—because we don't know what name I use," interjects Jeremiah.

"Identity papers for Callie. Again, with the name blank." Antoine is holding up fingers again. "Medical kit. Penicillin, antibiotics—every possible medicine we can put our hands on that might be useful."

"A list of all the battles of the Peninsular War and comprehensive notes on the movements of the armies, plus every major historical event of the last two centuries." Jeremiah waves a leather folio. "All carefully written in pen and ink on paper from that time, just in case anything from *this* time won't travel back."

My eyebrows lift. "The medicines?"

"We figured it was worth a shot." Antoine and Jeremiah exchange a grin. Despite everything, despite the heartwrenching gravity of what we're all facing, they both seem strangely excited.

"You're actually looking forward to this, aren't you?"

Jeremiah's smile fades as he sees my face. "Don't think that all this means I'm any less focused on what I'm going there to do, Harper," he says quietly. "I will do everything in my power to send your twins back. But if I'm not coming back with them . . ." He shrugs. "I guess I just want to give myself the best chance I can."

"I know that, Jeremiah." I fold my arms over my chest, feeling oddly cold. "But the thought of never seeing you—or Callie—again . . ." The tears that only recently dried threaten to spill again. *I miss Callie.* There's a sudden, painful ache in my chest. I miss her quiet watchfulness, her tough facade, her quirky mannerisms. I miss her strange mixture of wisdom and naivety, and the fiercely loyal heart that she shows to so few. Even the thought of never hearing her wry comments or seeing her reluctant smile again breaks my heart. And Jeremiah . . . I look at him, the grave features that have so much more maturity and depth than any man his age should, the lean frame that has somehow become hardened over this past year, the dark eyes that have already seen so much. If Connor has been my home, Jeremiah has been my brother through all this, for a long time the only ally I had to share my secrets with. He has long been family to me.

"I can't believe you're going," I say softly. "It's too much, Jeremiah." My throat closes over, and when Antoine comes to stand beside me and silently puts his hand on my shoulder, I don't move away, but cover it with my own. They continue to talk and I sit there, in the dim room, as they plan Jeremiah's new life, in a world two centuries apart from our own.

CHAPTER 16

MOMOY

It's evening when Tate and Iara join us. We've been talking all day.

There's a restless atmosphere in the mansion, a jittery excitement that for once isn't of my making, or reflected in the weather. We're all aware of what we are trying to undertake. It's both terrifying and, for Jeremiah, at least, exciting. I don't feel excitement. I'm not sure what I feel. I try not to think of all the things that could go wrong in those dark, chaotic pathways. The mere thought terrifies me.

"Harper." Iara comes directly to where I'm standing alone in the kitchen. "How are you feeling? Are you okay?" I turn to her and without thought, I'm suddenly in her arms, hers about me, and it is a long, silent moment of unspoken connection, of comfort and mutual understanding. I can feel Iara in a way I can't anyone else. When I'm near her, it's like a soothing layer of protection falls over me, a cocoon of safety between me and the world outside. I feel as if nothing bad can come to me while she is here. It's hard to believe that she was only my age when she became a vampire. She seems so much older, almost like a maternal figure. That perception disappears abruptly when I look at her, of course; Iara's lush curves and wicked, dark eyes are anything but matronly. If Cass's physique could shame a catwalk model, Iara's would make a monk rethink his vows. The fact that she is also entirely clueless about her own appeal only adds to it, I suspect. Although neither she nor Tate has ever confided in me, it's plain to anyone that their relationship has long moved beyond the platonic stage. I'm glad for them both. Tate deserves to feel happiness again, and Iara, I think, was made to love others. She has one of the most generous, warm hearts I know.

When we finally break apart, the sky outside is purple and gold, the first stars pricking the sky. "You seem better." Iara touches my face with her palm, her liquid brown eyes taking in every detail of my expression. "Calmer. Happier. This is good. Better for bringing back the babies like this, *si*?"

My mouth twists. "Do you really think we can bring them back?" I ask her the question I can't bring myself to ask anyone else. "Do you believe it's actually possible?"

"Of course I believe." Iara puts her arm about my shoulders. "Come out to the others," she says, pushing me ahead of her. "Listen to Tate. We have been working on it all, *querida*. We have much to tell you."

They are gathered on the back porch, sitting on a jumble of chairs and upturned crates, Tate, Antoine, and Jeremiah's heads all bent together, talking excitedly. They look up when we come out. Tate glances at Antoine, who nods. "So," Tate begins. He holds up a small leather pouch. "Inside here is what you know as jimson weed. We call it *momoy*. It's a member of the night shade family—highly toxic in the wrong doses, but in the right, a powerful hallucinogenic."

"I've heard of it." I nod. "Guidry used to talk of it." Antoine's face tightens when I mention Guidry's name, just as it had earlier, when he mentioned the bank draft to Lysette. Whatever reasons Guidry has for doing what he did, it will be a long time, I suspect, until Antoine forgives him. If ever.

For my own part, I don't care if I never see Guidry again. I might understand, in some way at least, why he did what he did. But I will never forgive him for two hundred years of friendship with Antoine in which he never once, in any way, hinted at what might come, nor gave us any chance to stop it. Some things are simply too great to forgive and Guidry's actions, for me, fall into that category.

I focus on what Tate is saying. "Jimson weed—momoy—has been used by my people in ceremony for centuries to facilitate visions and journeys into other realms. Plenty of messed up adolescents still chew the pods to get high." Tate grins. "Unfortunately, most of them know nothing about how to use such plants or how to prepare themselves in the right way for the visions they bring." He shrugs. "To be honest, when we were young, we weren't much different. More than once my friends and I sneaked off to try it out. I'm no stranger to its effects.

"When I touched the lotuses, Harper, I could sense the pathways within them, just as I could sense your children. But I knew I couldn't enter them; I could feel it." I nod. I already know this. "It was Iara who said I don't need to enter the pathways myself." He takes Iara's hand and she smiles down at him, leaning against his shoulder.

"Jeremiah is pulled toward the place," Iara says. "His body— his physical body—senses it. Smells it, feels it, sees it. Tate's connection is different. Is in the mind." She taps her head. "In the soul." She touches her chest. "And is from his ancestors, in the sky." She says this last bit matter-of-factly, as though it is an indisputable fact, and none of us contradict her.

"Me, I have some of this magic also." Iara nods, again as if her facts are immutable. "A connection with spirits who understand the pathways. Knowledge of how they can be navigated. Tate and I, we will take the jimson weed. This will take away the barriers of the conscious mind, between what *is* and what we believe there is *to be*." She looks around at us, her expression oddly reminiscent of Katiusca's. "Is two different things, you understand." Her stern tone makes me more consciously aware of the old shaman's presence inside me, the rich, potent water path that I am still becoming accustomed to. I realize, with a weird jolt, that the impatience I often find myself feeling now, the certainty in my own actions, come from him. It is a realization I tuck away for another time, turning instead to listen to Iara.

"Tate and I will drink a potion made of the jimson weed and mixed with some of the blood you got from Avery." She nods at me and holds up a remonstrative finger. "Not all the blood; Jeremiah, he also must take some of this. But not the jimson weed. He cannot be in other dimensions. His senses must be the most acute, the most aware, for it is he who will be traveling the pathways, and this is dangerous."

I shudder, unable not to think of my babies traveling those very paths. Antoine moves quietly to my side, slipping his hand into mine, and I know he understands.

"Tate and I will enter the water garden. We will connect ourselves to the lotuses and to each other. This we must do alone, you understand? It is a circle that must be made and must not be broken, no matter how you might wish to help." She casts a somewhat fierce glance at Antoine and me as she says this, making it clear to whom her warning is directed.

"But surely we can do something," I say, frowning. "Antoine has the medicine woman inside him. I have the power of Abatey and Katiusca. And besides all those things, Aurelia and Marguerite are our daughters. What stronger connection could there be?" By Antoine's folded arms and glacial stare, he shares my dislike of this plan.

"The blood is the connection. The blood *before* you became what you are now, Harper. Not since. Blood that was taken when you held the twins inside you, when you shared a body. The Indigo, unawakened."

"Wait." I interrupt her, glancing at Antoine. "You keep saying those words: *the Indigo*. Keziah used them too. She said the Indigo was a *'rare, powerful gift'*. But she never explained what it is. I think it's time you did."

"No." Iara's answer is swift and immediate.

"What do you mean, no?" Antoine's icy glare freezes a notch closer to arctic. "Whatever is running in Harper's veins, don't you think she should know?"

"I don't mean I cannot tell you." Iara brushes aside his hostility with an impatient wave, seeming not at all cowed. I'm struck again by how much she has changed. Not just since becoming a vampire, but since *I* became a vampire. She seems older, as if she holds more inside her than she once did. I wonder, in some observant part of my mind, if that is what motherhood is like—an inner expansion of sorts. Then I put the thought away and focus on what she is saying. "I mean," Iara goes on, "that I might be able to describe it to you, but to use it, this cannot be explained. Only felt." She turns to me, the hint of impatience rather more pronounced. "You hold Katiusca inside you," she says, frowning. "Draw on him now, to understand."

I turn away from them and close my eyes.

The water path within me that is *Katiusca* rushes to meet me, although that is not quite how it is. Katiusca's path is part of my own. I know this, have known it since my transformation, but it frightens me, like catching sight of your shadow in a dark alley. I know it's there. I know it can't harm me. But it feels like a stranger in my own body nonetheless. Calling it *Katiusca* is no longer correct, for Katiusca is Harper, and Harper is Katiusca, and both flow in my veins. But his being—that is difficult to let into my conscious mind. What he knew, I know now also, but the sensation of opening myself, making my inner soul vulnerable so Katiusca's being can bring knowledge to my conscious mind, feels uncomfortable. In the moments when I fought Keziah or used the Abatey to come back to myself, we were one, indistinguishable. But in this moment, there is no imperative, no hard urgency nor task to complete. It is a voluntary step into the connection, and I understand, in a strange way, that Katiusca's being still holds some autonomy, even within my own soul.

"Ask." Antoine murmurs behind me. "Ask for what you need to be shown." I realize that this is what Antoine must do every time he calls upon the medicine woman Atsila who lives within him. "You won't always need to do so," he goes on quietly. "But at the beginning, until your connection is entirely settled, ask."

So I do. *What is the Indigo?* I think. *Show me what it is. How to use it.*

"You have seen it already."

It is not so much that I hear a voice; rather, I understand what is being communicated. I see the midnight sea, upon which I once dreamed of light filling my body and then into which I tumbled when I fell through time. I feel its velvet depths, a sense of timelessness and infinite space that nonetheless has substance and form. I find myself in it and part of it, and feel, for a fleeting instant, the utter power of it. The thoughts, when they come to me, are neither mine nor Katiusca's, but ours, and I open to them.

The Indigo is thinking substance. It permeates and penetrates the interspaces of the universe. All that we are, all that we can be, all that can be conceived, is created by it. All beings can access it, though few understand their own ability to do so. What we think can be created by the formless stuff of the Indigo.

In my mind, the midnight sea surges and rises, changing shape. I see in it cars and planes, cities and factories, but there are also trees and animals and seeds growing from the earth.

Those born with the Indigo in their blood are linked to the formless, to the thinking substance. They embody it, carry it consciously in their veins. These are the "genies" who grant wishes, the "magicians" who wield magic without training. They are the creators, the builders of our material world, sometimes consciously, sometimes unconsciously.

I see faces I have only seen in the media, or in history books.

Not all Indigos know the arcane nature of their gift. But all know their power—and use it. Sometimes wisely, sometimes unwisely.

This is why the gift is dangerous.

My eyes fly open. The last thought comes to me in Katiusca's own voice, hard and stern, and I understand the warning he offers. "But what might I do with it?" I whisper aloud, looking around, half expecting the little shaman to suddenly appear.

But I know the answer inside myself. It lives there, in my soul.

Whatever you wish.

I turn back to the expectant faces. When I speak, I don't realize what I'm going to say until the words are forming themselves. "Unawakened," I say slowly, "the Indigo is a raw, formless power that can move through time and space unimpeded. It is neither contained nor directed but surges wherever thought takes it. That is why it is such a great gift; those who carry it are not bound to time, place, or space. That makes them powerful beyond measure. Particularly if they decide to consciously manipulate any of those things." I look at Antoine. "The blood we mixed before the twins were born holds the infinite capacity of the Indigo, which is why it can transcend the barriers of time and travel through the formless stuff of the universe. But as you already know, vampires are fixed. We cannot travel the paths ourselves, or at least, not through time. I can still dematerialize in this time, and place, for the indigo in my blood is still potent — but it is fixed now to this time, as I am.

"But the blood we mixed before I was turned is mingled with the fixed quality of your immortality. We know that intermingling had a special power, because it created new life with supernatural powers. It had some particular shape of its own, that we and the twins share. Now, even after my change, that old blood still lives within me—but now it is fixed in this time, for eternity, because of *my* immortality. That means the Indigo in this time serves as an anchor. It links us to the twins and can carry the girls to us. But we cannot travel to them. And if we tried, if we mixed the Indigo that is frozen inside me with the formless substance of its raw form, we'd break the fundamental laws of what the Indigo is and can do. We would be trying to mix the dynamic, raw form of the Indigo with its fixed expression."

Antoine is watching me intently. I can almost hear the cogs whirring in his brain. "So your ability to dematerialize and to regenerate the living world. To control the weather or have it react to you—isn't that the Indigo still at work? It's still a dynamic force within you."

"Within this space and time, yes. The Abatey within me is connected to the earth, which is indivisible from the Indigo, so the two work in me to constantly regenerate the other. But it is a static force now. Contained within my body, which is no longer alive. The Indigo runs through me. But it cannot take me into itself anymore, as it could when I was alive. Now I am fixed, immortal and unchanging. I contain the Indigo, but I can no longer *become* it."

I realize Tate is smiling at me. "For something that can't be explained," he says dryly, "I'd say that was a pretty good attempt."

"But if you contain the Indigo," Antoine says, frowning, "why is it Tate who can access the flowers, and not you?"

It is Iara who answers. "Because it is not Tate's body that travels." Her response is swift and sure. "Is his mind." She taps her head. "His spirit. It is his ancestors who carry him into this space. That is a force that has nothing to do with Indigo this, blood that." She waves a slightly impatient hand. "He travels not in physical form, though if his spirit is lost, his body will no longer matter, for in the end we are all only spirit. But for this journey, though he drinks the blood to help his ancestors find the link, he does not need his body to follow the paths, only his being. Tate is Natchez, made of this earth, his ancestors buried in it for generations. It is his ancestors who can be called upon here."

"Wait." Jeremiah has the same expression of concentration as Antoine, which makes my heart twist. "If the Indigo in you keeps regenerating, why was that not the case for Caleb?"

"Keziah didn't really understand that either." I shake my head. The time I spent with Keziah feels like a mist-filled dream during which I was neither who I had been, nor who I am now. It's uncomfortable to think of. "She thought it was because Caleb had drunk so much of their blood—of the three shamans —before he was made. But that wasn't it, was it?" I turn to Iara, who is watching me with dark, soft eyes, as if willing me to find the answers myself.

I love her so much.

"It's because Caleb craved their power," I say slowly. "That was what he saw in their Indigo, what drew him to them. It wasn't that they were inherently dark, nor that the blood inside them was. It was what Caleb *himself* desired when he drank from them. Caleb wanted their dark power. He thought it would make him the most powerful of them all. And with every part of the Indigo he took inside himself, he formed it into dark, deathly power—until that became all he was and all he could be. Darkness and death. He didn't understand that he was creating what he desired at every step." I frown, trying and failing to describe exactly what I mean. "This is the part that can't be explained." I say it slowly, only truly understanding it myself as the words come from me. "The Indigo is always exactly what we make it become. It is infinite and formless and becomes exactly what it is meant to be, created with every intention of the person wielding it."

With that thought comes a realm of possibility that I know I have only barely begun to understand. And with it comes hope. I meet Antoine's eyes. "The Indigo is not fixed," I say quietly, feeling an unguarded wellspring of happiness begin to unfold inside me. "It can be moved and shaped, can alter at any time." As I speak, a gentle breeze begins to sway around us. It is filled with the springtime scents I love: delicate redbud and heirloom roses, underpinned by the earthy power of dogwood and bayou mud. I turn toward the river, where the moon is rising behind thin gray clouds, and blow softly.

The clouds drift apart on my breath, and the moon shines through, golden, bright, and clear.

CHAPTER 17

PORTAL

When we begin talking again, I feel different. We are still in the garden, close to the pond. My hand is in Antoine's and, even though my babies are far away and the journey to get them is both dangerous and unknown, I feel lighter than I have since my transformation.

"So you will take the jimson weed." Antoine is repeating every step slowly, and I can feel him processing each from every angle, scrutinizing them for fault lines, turning every nuance of the plan over in his mind. His analytical brain is so at odds with Iara's instinctual knowing that if the process weren't so grave, it would be comical to watch them.

"Yes," says Iara impatiently. "I say this already." Like Callie, her accent becomes more pronounced the more impassioned she gets. "Tate and I, we take the herb. Some of the blood she is on the lotus; some she is in the mixture we drink. Some, Jeremiah also, he drinks."

"But Jeremiah is not in the water garden with you," Antoine interjects.

"Only at the beginning of his journey. He will enter the pathways in the water, but then—he will be gone." Iara reaches out to hold Tate's hand and I tense, glancing swiftly up at her. She meets my eyes briefly and looks away. Nobody else, I realize, saw what I did: Iara's fingers are trembling.

She's afraid, and that, more than anything up until now, sends bolts of fear down my spine.

"Iara." Her eyes meet mine with mingled defiance and resignation. "What will you and Tate do, once you have made a link to the pathways?"

Tate's fingers tighten on Iara's, but when he answers, his tone is light.

Too light.

"Jeremiah can't actually access the paths. So Iara and I will have to make—a portal, of sorts. A passageway down which he can travel."

Jeremiah coughs, more to remind us all he is still here, I think, than any other reason. "I already know this part," he mutters, glancing uneasily at Antoine. "I'm going to—" Gesturing awkwardly, he backs away, not meeting my eyes, and disappears into the house. He clearly knows exactly what Tate is about to say and has no desire to be anywhere close to the fallout that follows it. None of the others so much as register his departure.

"A portal." Antoine is staring at Tate, his eyes narrowed. "How do you make this portal?"

"We're not entirely sure." Tate meets Antoine's eyes with the same mixed expression as Iara. "What we do know is that the portal is held within the lotuses. We can both feel it, and we know we can open it."

"But you don't know how, exactly, this portal will open—or how to keep yourselves from falling through?" Antoine folds his arms, glancing around at the small group. "Do you actually know how to send Jeremiah into it? Or have any certainty as to where he'll end up?" His tone is becoming increasingly cold and angry. Antoine does not like unknowns. He is a man of plans and outcomes, goals and strategies. I can feel with every nerve ending how repellent he finds the idea of dealing with an unseen force, with an uncertain destination.

"Jeremiah is knowing this." Iara's voice is equally annoyed, though hers is expressed through her ever-thickening accent, the words coming as rapid-fire as bullets. "With the blood inside him, Jeremiah, he will feel the moment, *si*, when he must step into the water and pass through the flowers, into the portal."

"Pass *through* the flowers? He will *feel* it?" Antoine doesn't attempt to hide his disdain. "How, exactly, does he pass through this portal?" His face is a picture of skepticism, but I, having traveled those chaotic realms before, can feel a slow suspicion rising like dread inside me.

"This portal," I say quietly, looking between Tate and Iara. "Part of you will *become* it, won't you? It isn't something you make, as such. It's something your spirits become." When they don't speak, I know I'm right. "The jimson weed." I turn to Antoine. "It opens the spaces of their minds, so the Indigo in my blood can use the spiritual connection Iara and Tate possess with the land, their ancestors, and each other, to become what it needs to be, without their thoughts creating it. The blood will use their spirits to reach into the darkness, searching instinctively for its own stuff. And once the connection has been made between the blood here and the blood in the past, Jeremiah will touch the flowers and step into it with the intention of going from one to the other."

Antoine has gone very pale. He's staring at Tate. "But the twins are babies. They won't have the ability to form that kind of intention by themselves." His voice is oddly quiet. "They won't know what to do. And we already know that Jeremiah doesn't come back through that portal."

"No." Tate's voice is equally quiet. "We know that, Antoine. Which is why one of us will hold the portal, while the other will need to travel back to get them." I knew what was coming. Part of me, I think, has known it from the moment Tate said he could feel something in the lotuses. But knowing it is not hearing it. Knowing it is not the reality of the pain and terror in Antoine's eyes, the iron-hard tension of his body beside mine.

"One of you." Antoine's eyes gleam a savage, tortured crimson. "You. You mean that you are going to do this."

Tate's lips twist. "Who else, brother?"

"Iara said that if your spirit is lost, then your body no longer matters." Antoine's voice is flat and hard. "Which means that if you are lost in there, you are effectively dead, immortal body or not."

Tate doesn't answer.

"Harper." Antoine speaks without turning away from Tate. I don't need him to finish his sentence.

"We'll wait for you inside." Iara and I leave them facing one another on the grass and, barely a moment later, are in the salon. Wordlessly, we part ways on the stairs, she heading toward the room she and Tate use when they stay overnight, me to mine and Antoine's at the other end of the mansion. It's a false privacy, really. Distance is no barrier against vamp hearing, and I suspect Iara is about to do exactly what I am—perch on the window seat and listen shamelessly to the conversation in the garden below.

"No." Antoine's voice is hard and definite. I can see his figure clearly from the window: legs parted, hands clenched into fists at his side.

Tate laughs softly. "Yes." He doesn't flinch from Antoine's grim stance. "You said to me once that we are bound by ties of blood and family, and by a Maker's bond." I wince. I remember this conversation, remember the hard, unforgiving words Antoine had flung at Tate. "You and Guidry," Tate goes on unrelentingly, "you said you were brothers of the heart in a way you and I could never be."

Antoine makes a harsh sound. "I was wrong to say that. You know I was wrong. I didn't mean it—"

"Yes, you did." I sense rather than see Tate's expression. I know that twisted, pained smile well. "And you were right. I haven't been your brother. Not in centuries. And although I might like to blame you for that distance, the truth is that part of me never truly forgave you for what you did to Marguerite and me."

"Tate—"

"Let me speak." Tate steps forward, and the light from the mansion catches the hectic flush on his angular face that I recall from the night when Antoine had spoken so severely to him. "Whatever Guidry's motivations, he has been at your side all these years, unquestionably loyal."

"And he knew all along that I would lose my children and never once said a word!" Antoine's roar takes even me by surprise. He rakes a hand through his hair, and for once, there is not a trace of his customary control. "You were right." His voice trembles. "You warned me that Guidry knew more than he should, that he seemed unusually interested in my children. Don't think I haven't remembered your words every day since the twins disappeared. Don't think I haven't wondered why it is that in the seventy years before we all came together under Lysette's network, I saw Guidry perhaps a few times a year, maybe more when we were in the same country—while in the years after that time, we were as brothers, Guidry rarely far from my side. And I was arrogant enough to never so much as wonder at his unquestioning loyalty. Don't think I haven't wondered why it is that he has run away now. And not just run, Tate. Disappeared. Without leaving even the ghost of a trail." His face is grim with anger, his eyes flashing fire, and I realize how much this has tortured him, this betrayal by the man he had thought his closest friend.

"No." Tate cuts him off so sharply it cuts through Antoine's anger. "Guidry is bound by whatever strange laws govern the pathways of time, a victim of them as much as anyone. If he truly did live some of these events, it was centuries ago. *Centuries*, Antoine." Tate shakes his head. "He cannot have known how events would play out at this end of those years, no matter what he knew back then. If he had known, he would not have been so worried about whether we'd beat Keziah or how the night of Harper's transformation would unfold. Still, he stayed at your side. All these years, Antoine, he has guarded you, helped keep you safe, waiting for this one moment when he could help your twins be born and help ensure your safety. What is that, if not true friendship? True loyalty?"

"Then why is he gone now?" Antoine paces across the ground and back. "And don't tell me it's because of the damned *laws of time*. He still could have helped. I'd have forgiven him anything if he'd have just stayed—" He turns away abruptly, cutting off the rare show of emotion with a grim discipline that breaks my heart. "And all this time," he mutters, staring into the darkness, "you were there. My oldest friend and, for centuries, the only damned child of my blood in existence." His words are hard and unsparing, wrenched from a raw place deep within. "You have nothing you need make up to me, Tate. There is no loyalty you didn't offer. The fault is mine. Let me own it. And do not do this." When he turns back to Tate, the crimson rage is gone, replaced by a tortured darkness that is made painful to witness by my sensing how long it has festered within. "Do you know what Marguerite asked of me on her deathbed?" He grips Tate by the shoulders. "She asked me to reconcile with you. That she needed to know that we would be brothers again—and that I would take care of you. I knew she would never truly forgive me for what I did to you both. And I wanted to give her the promise she asked for. I did." His voice cracks, and he continues with an effort, the words broken and hoarse. "But I couldn't bring myself to do it. I couldn't imagine ever finding the courage to face you after what I'd done, imagine a world in which you would ever want me as your brother. And in some ways, since I met Harper, it's been even worse."

I freeze, every nerve attuned to his words.

"Now I know what you lost." Antoine's voice is a no more than a rasp. "I understand how it feels to have a part of yourself live inside another person. I took that one great love from you both. There is not a moment that has passed in the years since that I have not blamed myself for what I did. I have never told you how sorry I am for that." He lets go of Tate's shoulders and steps back, trembling with the effort to master himself. "Let me do so now."

"I know you weren't in control." Tate's voice is rough. "Whatever anger I once felt is gone."

Antoine's head comes up sharply. "I didn't turn you because I wasn't in control."

"Then why?" Tate's voice is raw, the old pain undimmed by the passage of time. "Revenge?"

"Christ, no!" Antoine closes the distance between them in one swift, preternatural movement, his hands gripping Tate's arms with a strength that makes the other man wince. "It was the most damned selfish act of my life, one I've never forgiven myself for. But never think I did it for revenge, Tate, or because I lacked control." His voice drops, the words barely audible even to my ears. "I did it because I couldn't face life without you. Because even if you hated me, at least my eternity would have you in it."

There is a long pause during which neither of them moves. A pause in which, I know, the axis of Tate's world is shifting, the reality he has assumed since the moment he woke as a vampire is blown apart, reassembled into a new shape.

When he finally speaks, his voice is unsteady. "I have discovered recently that it is possible to have more than one great love." He lifts a shoulder awkwardly. "That, perhaps, the love that comes with time and wisdom is the greatest of all. The one that comes when we know ourselves well enough to reach for it, instead of running the other way." He stares at Antoine. "And now I need you to make me a promise."

"Anything." Antoine's answer is immediate.

"Whatever happens," Tate says slowly, "I need you to promise me you will look after Iara."

Antoine is silent for a long time, and then his head drops. "Please, Tate. Don't do this."

"It has to be done." Tate's voice is hard. "And I need to do it. It is my task; I know this. My way of giving back the life I once took from you."

"I turned you because I could not face eternity without you," Antoine whispers. "Don't make me face it now, Tate." I have never heard this note in Antoine's voice before, the naked, almost broken pleading. "My children—now Jeremiah—please, brother. I can't lose you, too."

"You won't, if I can help it." Tate's words are oddly determined. "I have a reason to live, Antoine." He smiles crookedly. "More than one. More than I've ever had before." His smile fades. "I'll do everything I can to come back. But if I don't, Antoine—if I can't—"

"Then she will be my sister." Antoine grips his shoulder. "You have my word, brother."

They stare at one another for a long moment, then Antoine pulls Tate forward in a hard, brief embrace. The wind is rushing in my ears, and I can barely see for the tears in my eyes.

I turn away from the window and leave the two brothers to their final goodbye.

CHAPTER 18

RINGS

We all fall asleep in various parts of the house, and it is midmorning when I hear people stirring downstairs. Antoine spent much of the night with Tate, and he is standing at the window when I come out of the shower, his face still showing traces of deep emotion. I touch his arm and he leans his head briefly on mine, an unspoken admission of what I know he won't express in words. We stand like that for a time.

"It will happen today," he says eventually.

"Yes." We don't say any more for a while, then finally I move away and get dressed.

"I thought there would be a special moon—something." I smile half-heartedly at Antoine. "There always has been before. But this is a waning moon, usually a bad time for magic. It seems wrong, dangerous somehow, to be working without the moon's help."

"It is a different time where the twins are now. Perhaps the moon phase is different there. I could check." He pulls out his phone and begins to look it up, and I wave him away. "It doesn't matter, in the end." Realizing how hard my voice sounds, I smile in an attempt to soften it. "It has to happen today, either way."

We are quiet for a little longer, Antoine still staring out the window, and I know he is thinking of Tate and Jeremiah and what lies ahead. As much to change the subject as anything else, I ask something that's been eating at me. "Why are you so adamant that you won't give Avery what she's asked for?" I move to the window and he glances at me, unsmiling.

"If you're right about what's inside those pendants—"

I cut him off. "I'm sure I am."

"Then the blood is a link to them. One we're relying on being strong enough to pull the twins back through time. And if what your sister said is true, our daughters will be wearing that blood around their necks for the rest of their lives. It will be their guide, their anchor." His eyes when they meet mine are deep slate, the gold shards in them hard and unforgiving. "If it's that powerful, there's no chance in heaven or hell that I'm going to risk that blood linking anyone else to our children. Particularly not an emotionally unstable teenager who wants to be a wolf to get her boyfriend back."

The part of me that is Avery's friend wants to defend her. But the greater part of me shudders at the thought of my twins being magically linked to anyone else. Particularly an unknown creature, one we can't predict. And if we've learned anything these past few years, it's that none of us can be trusted in the time after we change.

"You had better be sure that Avery doesn't know that." I heard Jeremiah coming, so I'm hardly surprised, and his grim tone isn't much of a shock, either. He comes to stand at my side, so we're both facing Antoine, the river gleaming in the sun through the window.

"I'm not going to change my mind, Jeremiah." Antoine's tone is equally hard. I know that tone. Antoine won't bend on this, no matter the consequences. "Even if I trusted Avery—which I don't—I would refuse this. Not only because the process itself is both incredibly dangerous and unpredictable, but because nothing on this earth could induce me to create a magical link to our children that could one day be used to control or manipulate them. There's no way it's happening."

Folding his arms, Antoine fixes us both with hard eyes. "And neither of you is going to breathe a word of this to her until we've done all we have to do today, is that clear? I don't care how much of a good friend she is to either of you. Right now, your life"—he nods at Jeremiah—"is already in enough danger." He looks at me. "I don't need to tell you what's at stake," he says quietly. I slip my hand in his and nod. His fingers tighten briefly on mine, then release. "I need to go and organize those papers we spoke about." He nods at Jeremiah. "I'll be back shortly." He leaves through the window, jumping soundlessly to the earth below, and a moment later I hear his truck roaring down the driveway.

"You know," I say, staring unseeing down to the river, "if we're going to actually raise children, we're all going to need to learn to act more like humans. What if the twins think that leaping out the window is the right way to leave a house?" I turn back from the window to find Jeremiah watching me with a half smile. "I know." I shake my head. "But those are the things I think of, Jeremiah. They might be stupid, but they're also easier than thinking about sending you back through time—or never seeing Callie again." My voice breaks on the last couple of words, miserably trailing off.

I whip across the room and busy myself in a box I left beside the wall. I know what I'm looking for, but I'm also turning away so that Jeremiah won't see my face. Not that it matters; a sudden burst of rain spatters against the window, falling from nowhere. I might understand in theory that I can choose how to direct the Indigo in my blood, but I haven't yet mastered the art of doing so. And I don't want Jeremiah to feel any more worried about Callie than I know he already is.

"You don't know that you won't see her again," he says stiffly.

"Yes, Jeremiah. I do." I find what I am looking for and turn, forcing myself to meet his eyes with a small smile. "I know you find her, Jeremiah. And I know you both stay there, in the past."

Jeremiah freezes, staring at me. "Why? Has Antoine said something?"

"No." I look down at the velvet drawstring bag in my hands. "It's more . . . what he didn't say." I frown, trying to find the words. "I can sense things, Jeremiah. A lot of things, about what people feel, what they do and don't say. The first night we all talked about this, about you leaving, you asked Antoine about your wife. Do you remember?" Jeremiah gives a sharp, quick nod, his eyes intent on mine. "Antoine said that he *heard* you had a wife. There was something in the way he said it, a certain caution, that reminded me of how it was for me, when I got back from visiting Tessa—and of Guidry, when he tried to warn Callie of what to do."

Seeing Jeremiah's face harden at mention of Guidry's name, I say quickly, "There are things the water paths prevent us from speaking. It seems that one of those things are specific names— anything, I suspect, that might somehow complicate past and present timelines. I don't think Antoine doesn't know the name of your wife. I think he just can't say it."

"If it isn't Callie," Jeremiah says harshly, "that hardly matters, does it? And why haven't you just asked Antoine, if you suspect all this?"

"Because I know that if there was anything more Antoine could say or do to keep you safe, then he would have. There is nothing he wouldn't do, no stone he would leave unturned, if he thought it could help you. If he isn't speaking, then he can't." I take a step forward, the bag still in my hands. "But there was something Guidry once said to Callie," I say softly. "Something neither of them thought that anyone heard. I shouldn't have been listening, but I was. It was the morning before I gave birth to the twins. Guidry was talking to Callie below my window."

Jeremiah frowns. "I remember that. I came across them when Antoine sent me to find Guidry."

I half smile. Of course he would remember that. Jeremiah had always been hyperconscious of Guidry's proximity to Callie. "I didn't mean to listen in, but I was so heavily pregnant I found it hard to do much but lay down. Callie asked why Guidry was so sure she was the right person to remain at my side while I gave birth. Guidry said that he knew she was the right person not only for that task, but for *everything else* that lay before her." Jeremiah's eyes narrow. "And it wasn't just her. He was talking about you both. He said: *I believe you both have talents, Callie. Believe me when I say you will do extraordinary things together. Things that will change lives. Save them, too.* I pause. Jeremiah is pale, watching me intently. "And there's something else. At the time, I thought it was a just an oddity of Guidry's speech, as he's spent so long speaking in other languages. Now, though, I think it was an unconscious slip of the tongue.

"On the day Guidry told us about Madame Lysette and the *maison close,* he made Callie repeat the address. When she said all the details back to him, Guidry laughed and said: *You, my child, will make a superb spy.*" I take a step closer to Jeremiah. "Not, *would* make. *Will.* I don't think that was an accident of language, Jeremiah. I think that Guidry already knew what Callie would one day become. Antoine said that Guidry was heavily involved with Madame Lysette's network and with El Viajero. I think the reason Guidry found your jealousy and Callie's insecurity so amusing is because when he met you the first time, you were already married. And I think that on some level, Antoine knows that too."

Jeremiah is still silent, his eyes oddly fixed, exactly as Antoine's are when he is processing something inside. The similarity makes my heart ache. It makes me desperately sad that I will never see this again, this likeness between the two of them.

"Here." I hold out the bag in my hand. "Callie and I found

these together when I was still human. We were going through Tessa's and my things, boxes Mom had left to us, and we found this bag with two rings in it. Rings I swear I've never seen before." Jeremiah looks up suspiciously, and I can't help but smile. "I have no idea where they came from, Jeremiah. And this is one mystery I doubt we will solve—they turned up in a box of old family heirlooms, and there's nobody alive now who'd know anything about them. But Callie loved them. They seemed to mean something special to her. And weirdly, they're decorated with the fleur-de-lis—the symbol of the French Revolution." My hand closes over his, and I feel a bittersweet tug within at the connection. "I want her to have them, to have something of us with her always. Don't open it now," I say hastily as he takes the bag. "I'm already making it rain. Seeing you open that will likely bring Niagara Falls down on our heads." I give him a watery smile. "I think they're meant to go back with you," I say softly. "I think that in some strange way, they were always meant to be yours and Callie's."

Jeremiah is staring at the bag, his eyes hidden from me. "You're so certain that I will find her," he says, his voice breaking slightly, "that you're sending these back with me?"

"I've put a note inside the bag." I try to smile. "I even wrote it on that old paper of Antoine's, with the ink he used to write your bank documents, so it should survive the journey. I can't know if the rings will, but I have a feeling they are older than where you're going; and also, that they want to go with you." I shrug, realizing how odd it sounds. "I can't explain it. I just think they'll make it."

Jeremiah nods silently. His hands grip mine. He doesn't look up for a long time. When he does, I can see the tracks tears have made on his cheeks. He doesn't speak. Just presses my hands one last time, then leaves the room.

Rain falls softly against my window in a slow, steady stream, and it takes a long time to stop.

CHAPTER 19

APPALACHIA

Right at noon, Connor's truck hurtles down the drive. He and Cass are out and up the stairs before I've barely had time to register their arrival.

"We've got a problem." Cass takes my hand. "Avery is gone."

"I'd have thought that was anything but a problem," Jeremiah says wryly, folding his arms.

"You don't understand." Connor barely looks at Jeremiah. "Remy called early this morning. Seems Avery turned up there the day after she met with you two." He shakes his head. "It didn't go well."

"Didn't go well how?" I see Antoine's truck coming up the road and feel a warmth steal through my veins. I'm still getting used to the idea that we are in this together. Everything seems possible when I remember that. Even getting our children back from the past.

"Antoine's here. Good. I'll wait and tell you all together." Unusually, Connor actually looks relieved as Antoine's truck pulls up and he jumps out with the lithe grace that still, even after my transformation, makes my breath catch. Tate and Iara have come downstairs and are standing quietly off to one side. When Cass slips her hand into mine, I squeeze it gratefully.

"What is it?" Antoine asks without preamble, seeing Connor's grim face.

"Avery. She found out where Remy is and drove up there."

"Avery drove over seven hundred miles, up into the Appalachian Mountains of eastern Kentucky?" Antoine folds his arms grimly. "Why?"

"Wait." I look between them. "You knew where he was?"

"We knew." Connor barely glances at me. "Remy told us before he left, in case there was an emergency and we needed to contact him."

"You both knew." I look at Cass and she bites her lip and looks away. "Wait. You *all* knew? And you didn't tell Avery?"

"Remy wasn't quite telling the truth when he said he wasn't having dreams," Cass says quietly. "He was. He had been, for a long time."

"About someone else? Is that why he left?"

"No." Connor glances at me. "They were about Avery."

"Then why didn't it go well?" I look around at them all, and even Jeremiah looks away. "What is it you're not telling me?" For once my supernatural senses are of almost no use. I can feel their anxiety and trepidation, but I can't see what they're hiding.

"When Remy dreamed about her, Avery wasn't a wolf. Well —she was," Connor amends, "but she wasn't part of their pack. She wasn't like me, either. She was—something else altogether. Something dark. Dangerous."

"Like what?" I'm trying to understand what they're saying, but I can't.

Antoine rubs a hand over his face, shaking his head. "That's just it," he says wearily. "We don't know. Remy didn't know, or couldn't see. Even Connor and Remy, different as they are, can see something of each other when they are both in wolf form, and sense each other, to an extent, when not. And Remy said that he can feel pretty much all those in the bayou who have the wolf inside them, even before they've turned for the first time. But he never sensed it in Avery. And when he dreams of her, the dreams aren't like those that herald the Mating among others of their kind. When this girl, Bailey, came down from the Appalachians and started talking about how Mating works between wolves, Remy asked her, and the other wolves, about the dreams he was having." Antoine meets my eyes, and I can see the dark concern in his. "When he described what he'd seen in his dreams to Bailey, she was absolutely terrified. She wouldn't tell him why, only that he had to return with her and tell the others about the dreams."

"And that he couldn't say a word to Avery." Connor glances at me. "Bailey was super clear on that point. Whatever the dreams mean, Avery is in them—and not in a good way. That's why Remy left without telling her. And, I imagine, why he hasn't contacted her again. But somehow she tracked him down, and yesterday, she showed up in the tiny town where he's been staying."

"What happened?"

Connor shakes his head and exchanges a dark glance with Cass. "It's not good, Harper."

"Apparently," Cass takes up the story, "Avery told Remy about her plans to change into a wolf. Remy was—well, he rejected the idea pretty hard. He didn't tell us why, or what his dreams mean. But what Remy did say is that he told Avery that he would never agree to her changing, that it was *more dangerous* than she could ever understand. That no matter what you promised, Harper, he would ensure Antoine never went through with it. And it gets worse." Cass glances at Antoine. "Remy told Avery that Antoine would never agree to what she'd asked. He said Harper must have made the promise just to get the blood back, already knowing she wouldn't keep it. He said that you"—Cass nods at Antoine—"would never agree to putting Harper's blood inside somebody else, now that the twins are born."

Since that is entirely true, there isn't much I can say. I realize that I am oddly relieved. I hadn't been looking forward to that discussion with Avery. I guess at least this way, it isn't me who has to break it to her.

Then I look at Antoine. He's staring at Cass, a fixed expression in his eyes, his face ashen. "But Avery already knew that," he says hollowly. "Didn't she."

I feel a horrible, icy cold rush down to my feet, and an unseasonably dark cloud tumbles across the sun, turning the spring warmth to a dark chill that creeps across the ground from the edges of the garden. Cass nods slowly, crimson shifting across the bronze of her eyes. Connor shakes his head. "I'm sorry, Antoine," he says quietly, and despite the slight tension that often exists between the two men, I sense my brother truly means it. "I think the whole show she put on here was just to shake us all off the scent."

"Wait." Jeremiah's face is equally pale. "What does that mean? What is she planning?"

"She didn't give us back all of the blood." They all turn to me at the same time as the wind picks up, plucking new blossoms from the branches, and sending hard gray clouds across the sky. "She kept some of it. And she never intended for Antoine to change her into anything. She plans to do it herself."

"We don't know that—" says Connor, but his voice is drowned out as everyone begins speculating at once, talking over each other as they try to make sense of Avery's plans. Amid the clamor, Cass turns to Antoine and me.

"Remy said she asked him if he'd dreamed about anyone else. Remy told her the truth—that he hadn't. And because he loves her, and seeing her so heartbroken was killing him, he told Avery that he *had* dreamed about her—but that the dreams weren't normal, were something very dangerous. He told her he didn't want to see her get hurt."

I wince, remembering Avery's fury when she spoke about how everyone but her had faced a life-threatening transformation. "She wouldn't have liked that."

"She didn't. Remy said she was angrier than he'd ever seen her. He tried to get her to stay, but she took off in her car. He said the whole pack tried to find her scent, but that Avery seems to have just vanished into thin air."

Everyone else has stopped talking, listening to Cass instead.

"Well, brother?" Tate asks Antoine quietly. "What are you going to do?" His eyes shift to me. "If Avery does use that blood, especially while we're trying to work the magic—who knows what might happen? What if it confuses the pathways somehow?"

Antoine and I stare at one another. I can see the storm inside me mirrored in the tumult of his own eyes, feel his terror and fury like an answering tide. "We don't have time," he mutters hoarsely, holding my gaze. "We have to do this tonight, or it will be too late."

"I could go." Antoine blanches. "You know I could," I say. "I'm the only one who can dematerialize. I could be there and back in minutes."

"You don't know where she is. Or even where to start looking." Antoine is shaking his head. "And besides, by all accounts, Avery is more powerful than any of us really knows. I don't like the idea of anyone facing her without backup. Especially not you. And especially not tonight." His arm snakes out, pulling me hard against his side, and though the clouds overhead roil, the wind abates slightly and the air softens around us. "If there is one thing a lifetime of war has taught me," Antoine says, looking around at everyone, "it's that you can only fight one battle at a time. Our most important battle will be fought here, tonight. Whatever Avery is doing is a fight for another day." He looks down at me. "We can't risk losing this chance," he says quietly. "If we don't get our girls back tonight, we might never have another chance. Do you agree?"

My surge of relief is powerful enough to take me by surprise. I lean against him, my arms around his waist, and nod against his shoulder. "I can't lose them," I whisper. "Not again. But if Avery does use that blood—"

"I will be inside the pathways," says Tate grimly. "I won't let anything endanger your girls, Antoine, I swear it." His eyes flash with the savagery of the French soldier who lives inside him, and for once I'm glad to see it, grateful for that mercenary strength.

"And I," Iara says, Keziah's crimson shadow gleaming in her eyes, "will hold the portal open and guard it." She looks at me. "With my life, if I must," she says quietly, and the love between us surges back and forth, a tide that is immutable as the ocean itself, a bond I trust more than I do my own new being.

"Harper and I will make sure nothing gets close to either of you." Antoine glances at me and I nod.

"Cass and I will stand guard alongside you." Connor touches my arm gently. "I won't let Avery come anywhere near your girls, Harper, I swear it."

"Me, too." Cass smiles gently at his side.

Jeremiah looks around at each of us. "It's only a few hours until the sun drops. Iara says the magic is best worked at sunset. We should all get some rest."

We all nod, but no one moves. In the end, we go indoors, but we are all, it seems, reluctant to be alone. We spend the afternoon hours in quiet conversation or just sitting in companionable silence. In the midafternoon, Iara and I go together to make the herbal mixture.

"I have the *momoy*. We need only mix that with some of your blood and the petals and leaves from the lotus. It is not complicated, this mixture."

I think back to the complexity of the potion I made for Connor, the ritual beneath a moon. "Is not like a potion," Iara says, reading my thoughts with the uncanny perception I'm becoming more accustomed to. This instant comprehension of the other's thoughts is uncomfortably intimate at times. At others, it is achingly reminiscent of the bond I once had with Tessa. Either way, it is unmistakably the bond of family, and I am grateful for Iara's presence. "This, it performs a function. The magic is what lies in the water paths. The mixture is only to open us to the spirits and those pathways, not to transform the essence of who we are." She shrugs. "Is different than your potions."

I understand, but as we carefully harvest the leaves and petals from the lotus, taking only the ones Iara specifies, I can't help but feel the process should be more ritualistic. I worry that if I leave a single small detail unaccounted for, it may affect the outcome, and so I cut the leaves with extra care, coax the petals from the plant with exquisite tenderness. When the time comes to pour the blood into the glass jar Iara holds, I hesitate, staring at the rich ruby inside the test tube. It's the last of the unawakened Indigo, the last part of who I was that links my children to me. "Must we use all of it?" I look up to find Iara watching with soft sympathy in her eyes.

"You can hold back a little, yes. But we must use enough to activate the lotus petals, and we must also have a little to drop onto the flowers themselves. Tate and I will do this later."

"What do you mean, activate them?"

"You will see." Iara smiles and holds up an eyedropper. "I am thinking you may find it difficult, so I brought this to measure the blood in drops. Like this you can be sure there is a little left." I fill the eyedropper carefully. Once full, nothing but the merest traces are left in the tube. Holding the dropper over the jar, I squeeze the rubber top, releasing one drop at a time.

It doesn't take much, not even the entire dropper. Suddenly

the dark, velvety petals inside the jar seem to come alive; gleaming, tiny veins run beneath their surface as if an electrical current was racing around inside them. The petals glow with deep, rich colors of indigo, pink, gold, and purple, like the most potent of summer storms over the Mississippi River.

I squeeze the rest of the dropper back into the tube, but it rises barely a quarter of an inch. Not enough to do the same again.

"You won't need as much to activate the lotus in the pond." Iara smiles at me. "If you like, you can put a few drops away somewhere safe, before you give the blood to Tate and me." I nod silently, grateful she understands. I know it isn't enough blood to repeat this feat, that holding back any of it is no more than a token gesture. But at the same time, that blood is all that links Antoine and me to our children. I squeeze two drops into a small glass container and slip it into my pocket. I don't want to let it out of my sight.

I watch Iara mix the potion slowly and then screw the lid on. "Tate and I will drink soon," she says. "Jeremiah later, just before he goes into the water. He knows what to do." She clasps my hands. "It will work, *querida*. I believe this. I do."

I can only nod. I have to believe her; the alternative is simply too dark to contemplate.

The hours pass slowly, every one seeming heavier than the last.

CHAPTER 20

PATHS

Dusk comes in a chorus of birdsong and a sense of jittery excitement.

"It's time." Iara looks across at Tate, then around at the rest of us. "The first part, Tate and I, we must do alone. To drink the herbs and weave the magic to open the water paths, yes? Keep your distance until we are in the water. Jeremiah, you know already what to do." Jeremiah nods soberly. He, Tate, and Iara have spoken at length about how this works. They've left Antoine and me out of those conversations. Our job is to keep them safe, not to be part of their magic. I'm trying to be okay with that.

Trying.

"No matter what," says Iara sternly, looking directly at me, "none of you will enter that water. Not for any reason, no matter what you see."

"You've said this." Antoine is leaning against the doorframe, arms and legs crossed, his face stony. "We understand."

"Make sure you do." Iara fixes him with a crimson hard eye. "Particularly you, yes? You will not enter that water, or you will risk everything." Antoine makes an impatient noise and turns away, but not before he's nodded his agreement. He hates this role as much as I do.

Tate pauses beside Antoine as he reaches the doorway. Putting his mouth close to Antoine's ear, he mouths something not even vamp hearing can pick up. Antoine nods grimly, his mouth a tight, hard line. His hand grips Tate's shoulder briefly, but he doesn't speak. They have said all that must be said, I know, just as I know they are both shifting into warrior mode now, where emotion plays no part.

Cass and Connor look at each other. "We will take up position by the river," Connor says quietly. "When you need us, we will be there."

Cass goes over to Jeremiah and puts her arms around him. "Don't forget us," she murmurs. "And give my love to Callie." Jeremiah nods jerkily but doesn't speak. She steps away, wiping hastily at her eyes. Connor puts his hand out and Jeremiah grips it. "Good luck." Connor's voice is rich with all he isn't saying, his vivid blue eyes so bright they shine like sapphires. "I'll miss you, Jem. We all will." He takes a deep, steadying breath. "This is for Callie." Smiling crookedly, he presses a small leather book into Jeremiah's hand. "It's old enough to travel, Antoine tells me. I've written all I know about our father's family in it—what little there is. There's a note from me, too. But I wondered if I could ask you to tell Callie something, from me." He pauses, swallowing hard, but when he speaks, his voice is quiet and sure, and he looks right at Jeremiah. "Tell my sister," he says quietly, "that I love her. And that I will never, ever forget her."

Jeremiah nods, gripping Connor's hand hard enough that their knuckles turn white. "I'll tell her," he says roughly. Connor nods and my heart twists. I see him long ago, in Tessa's room, his hands on hers, the words of goodbye stuck in his throat, unable to be spoken.

He has learned from that. We all have, I guess.

Connor turns away, but not before he meets my eyes, giving

me a half smile and a quick nod. I press his hand as he passes. *I'm so glad,* I think, but don't need to say. *I'm so glad there are no words left unsaid, no regrets to carry.*

We are left standing in the dim light of the salon, Jeremiah, Antoine, and I. Jeremiah comes forward, stumbling slightly as he reaches for my hands. "I'll make sure they come home to you, Harper," he says hoarsely. "I promise I will."

"I know, Jeremiah." I squeeze his hands, trying to smile. "I know you will. You're the bravest of us all, you and Callie. I think you always were." I put my arms around him, holding the lean, strong body close to my own, feeling the trembling tension and rapid thud of his heart. "Thank you for being my friend, Jeremiah," I whisper in his ear. "I could not have lived these years without you. And I can never thank you enough for all you have given us." Stepping back, I hold his face in my hands. "You've got my gift for Callie." His head nods in my hands. "Tell her—" I can feel my voice beginning to fail me, and I clear my throat, desperate to get through this without crying, for Jeremiah's sake. "Tell her thank you, for taking my girls when I could not. For sacrificing everything to keep them safe." I force a watery smile. "But most of all," I whisper, "tell her that I know she will live an extraordinary life, Jeremiah. I can feel it. I always could. And tell her I will always be there, whether she can feel me or not. Every time the wind blows or the rain falls, I will be among it, in the water paths, listening. I love her. I love you both. I always will."

He hugs me for a long time. Then he turns finally to face Antoine, his eyes dark caverns in his face. I go to leave them alone, but Jeremiah's hand shoots out and touches my hand, wordlessly asking me to stay.

"Well." Antoine's arms are folded. He nods quietly, the ghost of a smile on his face, there, then gone again. "It's time, then."

Jeremiah takes a sharp breath. "It's alright." Antoine touches him gently on the shoulder. "We don't need big goodbyes, Jeremiah." His eyes glitter oddly. "I know the man you are," he says quietly. "And even if I had never met El Viajero, I already knew that you were destined to become the very best of men. I have no right to say I am proud of you. But I can say that I am proud to know you; and that I love you, very much." His voice roughens on the last words but he gets them out, then swallows hard. "I'm more grateful than I have words to express, or than you can ever imagine. Not just for this greatest of sacrifices." He meets Jeremiah's eyes steadily, his own grave and dark as a midnight sea. "But for giving me a life I could never have imagined. I would not be here without you. None of us would, Jeremiah."

Jeremiah stares at him, and when he finally speaks, his voice is rough as old wood, wrenched from deep within him. "Whatever man I am, or will become, is what you made me. Anything inside me that is good has come from you." Antoine's eyes flare, gold shooting through the midnight blue like a full moon over water. "I know that you will be the best of fathers to those little girls." Jeremiah's mouth twists. "Because nobody could have been a better father to anyone than you have been to me. I will never forget you." Antoine pulls him into a hard embrace, and Jeremiah grips him with all the lean strength in his body.

"I will see you again, Jem," Antoine mutters, holding the younger man's head in one large hand. "I will see you again, I promise."

"I know." Jeremiah's arms tighten. "But just in case you don't. I love you, Antoine. You should know that."

"I do." Antoine grips him briefly and then lets him go. "Now you listen to me, El Viajero." His mouth twists, and Jeremiah ducks his head, his own lips curling, and they look so much like a matched pair it breaks my heart. "It's time for you to go and find that girl. Marry her. Live an extraordinary life." He tucks a leather folder into the bag at Jeremiah's feet. "The papers I promised you." He winks. "And some notes regarding things I forgot to mention. For example, a reminder to make sure you buy a case of 1796 Augier Cognac. Trust me," he says, as Jeremiah begins to laugh. "You'll thank me later."

And that is how we go to meet the water paths of the past: laughing, our arms entwined, stepping toward the setting sun.

…

The sun is an orange ball across the river, turning the water the color of flame. Connor and Cass are standing on either side of the jetty, tense and ready. Cass is holding the jar containing the potion we mixed earlier, and as we draw close, she holds it out toward Jeremiah.

I look at the pond and frown. Even my supernatural eyes are having trouble assimilating what I'm seeing. Eventually I realize I'm not imagining it; but the realization doesn't make it any easier to understand.

The two lotuses are wide open, petals unfolded and gleaming rich indigo in the dying sunlight. I don't need anyone to tell me Iara has used my blood to activate them. Color ripples across the petals like an iridescent oil slick. The same electrical effect I witnessed earlier is even stronger in the flowers themselves, light gleaming in the stalks beneath the surface of the water like two beacons of subterranean light.

But it isn't just the flowers that are startling.

Iara and Tate are sitting cross-legged on either side of the lotus plants. Both are touching the outside petals of the lotuses with one hand, while their other hands are joined. There is a gap between them that I know is for Jeremiah. But it isn't their closed eyes or their otherworldly stillness that is striking.

They are cross-legged on the surface of the pond itself. Iara and Tate are sitting *atop* the water.

I glance at Antoine, who shakes his head. "I don't know either," he murmurs. I look at the ground. Barely two feet from where we are, the earth begins to soften, leading into my night garden and then to the pond.

"This is as far as we can go," I say, leaning down to touch the ground. "Any closer and we will be in the currents connected to the pond." Antoine nods. He threads his fingers through mine, and I can feel the tension in his grip, the rapid thud of his heart mirroring my own. Jeremiah turns to us from the jetty, the sun behind him so I can't see his eyes, but when he raises the jar toward us I smile, knowing it is his own farewell.

"Go well," Antoine murmurs beside me, watching with me. "Go safely, Jem." I squeeze his hand and he returns the pressure. I know Antoine feels as I do—that this much we can do, let Jeremiah know we are with him to the last.

Jeremiah hoists the bag onto his back, the straps over his shoulders and tied across his chest. I've told him all I can about the turbulence of travel through those pathways. He isn't taking any chances. He steps toward the pond, his eyes glued to Tate and Iara's prone figures. He hesitates for a moment at the water's edge; then he steps in.

I release a breath I didn't realize I was holding. Jeremiah doesn't walk atop the water, and I am strangely grateful that he doesn't. I sense he needs to be in the water, not apart from it. He wades carefully to the other two. His eyes are easier to see at this angle. They have become oddly unfocused, and in their depths, I see the shadow of the Indigo, creating a shimmering, otherworldly dimension to their darkness. Jeremiah stops. He is no longer looking at us or anywhere outside the pond; his attention is solely focused on the flowers in front of him. He reaches out with both hands and takes hold of each lotus, just beneath the surface, where the stems join the flowers.

There is only enough time to know that much, no more. Jeremiah is there, holding the flowers, tall and lean and silhouetted in the dying sun.

And then he is gone. Just gone.

The only trace of his presence is a slight shiver on the surface of the water and the two lotus flowers, which seem to pulse with an odd life. Antoine gasps beside me, and our clasped hands tighten—each of us, I think wildly, ensuring the other doesn't race toward the pond. Tate and Iara sway, as if they are both buffeted by a wind we cannot see. The sun slips behind the river, and we are in a deceptive twilight, the two figures in the pond suddenly seeming more distant, less clear, than only a moment before. I narrow my eyes. It isn't my imagination. The two figures *are* less distinct. A strange mist is rising from the water, first turning the two figures to shadow, then thickening to a swirling, silvery shroud through which nothing can be discerned. All around, the dusk is still, but from the mist comes snatches of sound—voices, speaking words I can't understand. A sharp cry of alarm. Strange whispers and fragments of conversation, muffled and indistinct, then startlingly loud and close, so I can't tell from which direction they come. As the mist wends through the garden and between Antoine and me, it brings not only the voices but scents: lavender and rose, onions and garlic, cooking and fresh washing. Callie's voice, sharp with fear: *They're gone!*

Callie's voice.

My heart leaps and seizes at once. *My babies. My babies are gone.*

I strain to see through the mist, feeling Antoine beside me twist and turn in the same effort, our hands fiercely clasped together. "Stay with me, Harper," he calls over the sounds. "Stay with me."

"I'm here, Antoine." I hold his hand tightly. "I'm here."

Harper! I hear Callie's scream, full of fear and hope. *Harper! If you can hear me—call them! Call them by their names!*

I turn to Antoine as he does to me, and as our hands clasp in the gloom, I feel a bolt of power lick between us, a knowing that transcends time, so that when I open my mouth to cry I know he will feel it too, and we cry out together: "Aurelia! Marguerite!" Antoine's roar and my cry blend and mingle, echoing into the distance, and he tightens his grasp on my hands. "Aurelia!" we call. "Marguerite!"

The names ripple and roar, over and over, echoing down the pathways into eternity, to become a long, continuous sound that seems to permeate every part of the world around us, vibrating in my very soul.

And then, suddenly, abruptly, the world is silent and still.

Something is wrong.

I know it. I can feel it. The mist around us is dense and thick, but it is no longer moving. There is no sound at all, just a terrible, deathly silence. If it weren't for Antoine's hands still gripping mine, I wouldn't know that he was there at all. Then his voice cuts the silence.

"Takatoka!" The cry comes from the depths of his soul, from the place within us all that we never wish anyone to know. It is a cry of terror and of pain. Then it comes again, but this time it's a cry of something else, something I have never truly known from Antoine. It is a battle cry, a sound from his past and from the man he once was, and it sends a tremor of fear down to the base of my spine. *"Takatoka!"* he roars.

Brother! Tate's answer comes through the mist, fierce and furious, and Antoine's hands on mine press so hard I've gone numb. *Brother! She's here! Avery is trying to take—Call them! You have to call them—*

Something cold and reptilian touches my skin. It feels smooth and insidious, and I can feel it trying to find an opening into my body.

Harper.

A cold, eerie voice whispers in my ear, making me shudder. It sounds like Avery—but also like something different, something detached and inhuman, with none of Avery's tension and emotion.

Harper.

"No!" I scream into the dense void. "Avery! I know you can hear me. Leave them alone. Leave my girls *alone!*"

"Don't let go, Harper!" Antoine roars, the sound ripping through the mist. "Call with me. The girls first, then Takatoka."

I draw my breath and our voices cry out into the darkness. "Aurelia! Marguerite! Takatoka!"

I can still sense the strange presence, like a cold shadow reaching for me, but our voices keep it at bay.

Avery! Far away, as if it comes from the far end of a tunnel, comes Jeremiah's voice, sharp and fierce. *A! This isn't you! Leave them, Avery, leave them alone . . .*

Through the shifting light comes a voice that is unmistakably Avery's, tearful and uncertain. *Jeremiah?*

Go, Avery! Leave them! Jeremiah's voice is fading, and as it does, Callie's comes again, sharp and high. *Call them, Harper. You have to call them—now!*

"Aurelia! Marguerite! Takatoka!" Antoine and I call their names, over and over, and then, from the very edges of the mist, other voices begin to chant with us. I hear Connor's voice, deep and strong: *Aurelia! Marguerite! Takatoka!*

Then Cass's, sharp and high and full of crimson rage: *Aurelia! Marguerite! Takatoka!*

On the very edges of reality, but nonetheless strong and clear as if she were beside me, I hear Tessa: *This way, girls. Come home. Come to me . . .*

Then a sweet echo that comes from the earth itself, a softer, fainter voice: *Takatoka . . . Antoine needs you . . . Come home.* I know, with a strange, beautiful certainty, that it is Antoine's sister Marguerite, calling her love back home.

"Aurelia!" The voices are growing stronger, and a shard of sunlight pierces the gloom. "Marguerite!" I can feel the earth warm and reassuring beneath my feet. "Takatoka!" The shard of sunlight tears through the mist like a sword, widening enough for me to realize it is the final, golden thread of the fallen sun on the horizon that is piercing the mist, and as the gap widens, I suck in the fresh night breeze like a benediction. I can see the pond, the first stars in the cobalt sky, and the two flowers, pulsating and glowing with a deep violet light more brilliant than any natural thing.

Then I realize there is only one clear figure still sitting there. Where Tate previously was, his body remains, but it is less substantial, as much mist as it is human form. Iara has a hand on both flowers and she's chanting something I can't hear. "Call them!" I scream. I can feel it; I can feel how close we are, see it in the pulsating flowers. Cass and Connor, their hands also joined, are looking at Iara, then at us. As one, we all chant the names together.

Aurelia! Marguerite! Takatoka!

The cries come from the deepest part of us all, and they echo around the garden, making the river water swirl and eddy. The flowers glow unbearably bright, so vivid that they are blinding —and then, suddenly, they explode into a million shimmering, diamond shards of light. I gasp and turn my face away, still holding Antoine's hands, terror racing through me. When I open my eyes, night has fallen, and all is blackness.

A sharp cry cuts the night, high and clear. Then a second.

Terror and hope choking my throat, my heart beating so fast I can barely find breath, I turn back toward the pond.

Standing in the water, face blazing with triumph, is Tate.

And he is holding in his arms two babies.

Our children have come home.

MIRACLES

My supernatural speed seems gone. My legs feel numb, clumsy, and all I can see are the two tiny, swaddled bodies in Tate's arms, two matching pairs of piercing blue eyes staring at me from the pond as I stumble toward them, my arms outstretched, the reality of their presence a miracle that feels as if it could disappear at any moment.

"Get out of that water!" Antoine roars behind me, his voice still fraught with tension. Tate meets me on the bank, and then my babies are in my arms, and I don't know how, but I'm sitting on the warm, dry earth, inhaling their sweet, holy scent and saying their names over and over.

Over their heads, I see Antoine gripping Tate in a fierce embrace and reaching to pull Iara from the water with his other hand. My Maker falls exhausted to the ground, her hand reaching for Tate's. I'm vaguely aware of Cass and Connor close by, flitting in and out, clearly still on guard and wary; then Antoine is touching my shoulder, his face still ravaged with emotion.

"Come inside," he says, glancing around warily. "We don't know if it's safe."

In the salon, I sit on the chaise longue and lay each of my babies down, so I can undo their swaddling. I need to see them, to know they are truly here, that I am not dreaming. I hear Antoine come inside and gently close the door behind him. I'm grateful. I need this moment of privacy, with just him and me and our children.

"They have your hair," I breathe, as I reach for the cloth with trembling hands. "And their eyes are like yours too."

"I think they are more like yours. They're blue, but like the blue underwater, when the sun hits it." He stops. "I'm babbling," he says shakily. "And anyway, it's too early to tell their eye color, isn't it?" Antoine's voice is uncharacteristically uncertain, and when he puts a hand on my shoulder, it trembles as much as my own.

"I guess so. I don't really know." One of the babies squirms on the chaise, crying out. I pick her up, and as I unfold her swaddling, the pendant that is around her neck and tucked inside it falls out. The filigreed silver is bright, seems almost to shine with an ethereal light, while the blood inside the glass vial beneath it glows and shifts like a living thing, strange colors moving in its depths. The baby grasps it in one fat little fist, and my first instinct is to seize it; but then she gurgles contentedly, her little legs kicking, far more strongly than I would have imagined in a newborn. She reaches for me with the other fist. I catch it with my own and feel an odd bolt of awareness in my blood.

"Aurelia," I breathe, unaware until I speak it that I know it is her. "This is Aurelia, Antoine."

"I know." He is staring at me, his brow slightly creased, and he holds up the swaddling I have just taken off. Stitched clumsily into the fabric in blue thread is the initial *A*.

"Callie," I whisper, tears clouding my eyes. I pass Aurelia carefully to Antoine, who takes her with so much terror on his face that it makes me smile through my tears. I reach for

Marguerite. She is quieter than Aurelia, her body seeming more tense, and when the swaddling comes away, I see, to my surprise, a blue *T* stitched inside it. I look at Antoine, but he shrugs, and I guess that I might never know what my daughter was called, back in that time. Marguerite reaches for her pendant, giving a soft little gasp as she touches it. She looks up at me through wide, cautious eyes that slowly soften, then her little body relaxes slightly. Antoine and I sit beside each other on the chaise, passing the babies back and forth, exclaiming over every small detail, from tiny toenails to delicate fingers.

"Do they seem . . . pale to you?" Antoine is examining Aurelia's skin worriedly.

"I don't know." But I do. He's right; I just don't want to say it aloud. Marguerite's skin feels paper thin, dry, and hotter than it should be, as if she has a mild fever. I stare worriedly at Antoine. "Do you think they're sick?"

"Something isn't right." Antoine himself is pale, his face drawn with the same fear I can feel in mine. "Look at Aurelia's eyes. They seem dull, somehow. And it feels like they're fading."

"What if they aren't meant to be here, Antoine?" Fear grips my chest. "What if they can't survive in this time?"

"We're not going to panic, Harper." The grim note is back in Antoine's voice, and it makes me even more afraid than I already feel.

Then Marguerite starts crying, a thin, high wail that is unmistakably a cry of hunger. Antoine and I look at each other, our fear mirrored in the other's eyes.

"There's the formula we bought," Antoine says. "Should we try that?"

I nod, unable to speak from fear. We take the babies into the kitchen. Balancing Aurelia on one arm, Antoine reaches for the tin of formula. "I should have read these instructions before," he mutters, and in other circumstances I would smile at his obvious annoyance at his own oversight. But right now, all I'm really seeing is the light fading from Marguerite's eyes, her list-less movements. I can hear Tate and Iara talking with Connor and Cass out on the back porch, but as yet, they're giving us space, and I'm grateful. I can hear Avery's name being discussed, but I don't want to so much as think about that right now.

The microwave pings and Antoine gingerly tests the formula on his wrist. He looks at me, frowning in frustration. "I have no idea if this is too hot or not," he says brusquely. "Why are their instructions so damned useless?"

"Here." I take the bottle impatiently and test it on my own skin. "It's fine." I tip the bottle up, but it barely touches Marguerite's lips before she cries out and feebly pushes it away, clearly disinterested. Antoine and I stare at each other worriedly. He reaches for the bottle, and tries to bring it to Aurelia's mouth, but she pushes him away even more forcefully.

"It's because they've been fed by that woman," I say, and the tears are back, making my voice shake. "They're used to real milk, not formula. What are we going to do, Antoine, if they won't feed?" I can feel panic and inadequacy rising like a red tide, and in the darkness outside the window a restless wind begins to blow, making me even more upset.

"Wait." Antoine's face has a fixed frown. "When you time traveled with the twins before, you came back thirsty, do you remember? You drank so much water I thought you'd drown in it."

"They can't live on water, Antoine."

Antoine's mouth twists at the corners. "You don't know that." Picking up another of the bottles, he fills it from the filtered water tap. He has barely brought it within reach when Aurelia grasps it fiercely, her mouth latching on to it and gulping the liquid down so rapidly I can watch the level drop. I take another bottle and fill it, and Marguerite does the same.

The infants take bottle after bottle, more water than seems even possible for such small frames.

"Look at their skin," Antoine breathes. Slowly, like a building dawn, rose is stealing back into their skin, turning it to a soft, pearlescent glow. As I watch, their eyes slowly deepen and darken, turning from a faded, washed-out blue to the clear, vivid color they returned with. By the time they finally push the bottles away, their skin feels dewy and moist, their limbs plump and soft, with none of the listless heat of only moments ago.

"Water." I shake my head. "Surely they'll need more than that to survive?"

"Maybe." Antoine's mouth twists in a crooked smile that warms my heart more than anything at that moment. "But who knows, Harper? And at least I won't have to navigate the damned powder stuff."

I laugh; I can't help it. After living with the unbearable tension of the past weeks, I feel almost giddy with relief. My small burst of laughter makes Marguerite gurgle with delight and clutch at my hair, which in turn makes Antoine chuckle. A moment later, we are both laughing, a little too loud and a little shakily, the laughter of those who have faced the worst possible outcome and somehow, magically and incredibly, survived.

It is then that the others finally come to the kitchen, crowding around us, cooing and laughing, touching the small faces with wonder. Antoine throws his arm over Tate's shoulders in a rough embrace, passing him Aurelia, and I have to look away when I see the tears glistening in Tate's eyes, his mouth unable to form words for emotion. I pass Marguerite to Connor, who takes her with the same mingled wonder and terror as Antoine had, making me smile and cry at once. Iara slips her hand into mine and I rest my head on her shoulder.

"Thank you," I whisper in her ear, so only she can hear it. "Thank you so much for bringing them back." Iara's eyes glow and she squeezes my hand, but she doesn't speak. I can feel exhaustion in every inch of her body.

Antoine turns to Cass, who is hovering on the edge of the

gathering. Taking Aurelia from Tate, he holds the baby toward her. "Would you like to hold her?" Cass's eyes shift to me, uncertainty and defiance warring in their crimson depths.

"I'm not sure that's a good idea—" Connor begins, and Cass stiffens, ready to flee.

"Yes, it is." I smile and nod at Antoine, who is standing right in front of Cass. She looks up at him nervously.

"Are you sure?"

Antoine nods. "I'm sure." He holds Aurelia out, and before Cass has time to refuse, the baby reaches for her, gurgling happily as her little fist twines in Cass's braids.

"Oh!" Startled, Cass takes the squirming figure and stares at her, fascination shimmering in her eyes. Aurelia touches Cass's face, then makes a contented little sound, settles in happily against her, and promptly falls asleep. "Oh," says Cass again, but this time in a soft tone of wonder. "My goodness. She's actually asleep."

Connor grins at her over Marguerite's head. "Looks like Auntie Cass just won babysitter of the year." He hands Marguerite back to Antoine. "But when it comes to diapers, you're on your own, buddy, no offense."

"Diapers?" Antoine raises his eyebrows at me. "Do they need those?"

"Do they *need* those?" Tate shakes his head, grinning. "Seriously?"

"Well, but that's the thing." Antoine and I talk over one another as we tell them about the babies drinking water and not milk, and how they changed when they did. Though we all talk it through, pondering what the reasons might be, we come to no definite conclusions. The subjects of these discussions have fallen asleep, Marguerite in my arms, Aurelia cradled easily in the crook of one of Antoine's. It is both incongruous and utterly natural to see him so at ease with a baby in his arms. I had never imagined it would make me feel like this, like I'm living a miracle.

As if to remind me of the mercurial nature of my reality, Iara says quietly, "We are needing to speak of Avery."

Silence falls across the kitchen instantly, all eyes turning to her. I realize again, with a pang, how utterly exhausted Iara is. Her eyes are dark caverns, marked underneath by noticeable shadows, and she seems thinner, as if there is simply less of her than there was before she went into the pathways. Antoine frowns. "You need to feed," he says abruptly, then, turning to Tate, "You, too. You're both starving."

"*Si, si.* Soon." Iara waves him away impatiently. She turns to me. "But for now, I must tell you what I saw in the pathways."

CHAPTER 22

SERPENT

The night is deep, the babies are sleeping, and we are strewn around the kitchen, me at the scrubbed pine table, Antoine leaning against the sideboard behind me. Tate is leaning against the sink, Iara at his side. Connor and Cass are standing by the door leading out to the porch. All eyes are fixed on Iara.

"The portal, she opened as I expected." Her accent is heavier, as it always is when she's tired. "And Jeremiah—this part, it was so easy. He was gone, straight to where the babies were, immediately." I nod, recalling how fast Jeremiah disappeared.

"I followed him," Tate takes up the story. "It was a strange sensation. My body was linked to Iara's through our joined hands, so it was only the spirit part of me that traveled into the darkness. I could feel Jeremiah, sense where he was going—and the blood, too, drew me onwards." He nods at me. "I could feel it, Harper. The part of you that was there, with the twins, was like a magnet, or mercury, wanting to join with what was within me. I felt as though I was being literally pulled by an invisible cord."

Iara folds her arms across her chest, shivering slightly. "It was hard," she says, "to hold him. Was like the past was pulling him toward it. I am having to work very hard, to keep him anchored, and I am beginning to be afraid that I am not strong enough." She shivers again. "I should have thought of this," she says, almost to herself. "That there should be more than one. So much force on one side, only me on the other." Looking around at us, she waves a hand dismissively. "Anyway. Then, I am feeling Tate reach the end."

"I couldn't see it," Tate adds. "I couldn't see anything. But I could sense it, like hearing voices behind a screen, so close I could touch them. I heard a clatter, like something crashing. I think it was Jeremiah, because they all called out in surprise, and I think I heard someone say his name. And then I heard Marie Roux." He shakes his head. "It was so strange. It's been more than two centuries since I heard that voice, but I knew it at once, as if it were yesterday. She called out the word, *now*, and as she did, I heard Callie, as if she was standing right beside me. She yelled out to Harper."

"I heard that!" I remember it clearly. "She told me that if I could hear her, I needed to call Aurelia and Marguerite to me." I look at Antoine. "You heard that, too, didn't you?"

"No." Antoine shakes his head. "I didn't." Connor and Cass also shake their heads.

"No," Iara says slowly. "This, I am thinking, is the blood link, Harper."

"I felt the babies," Tate says slowly, his eyes faded in his face, as if they have gone within. "I could feel them. But I couldn't say how. They were just with me, though I wasn't physical—and it seemed they weren't either." He gives a slight shrug and looks up at me with a wry smile. "I can't explain it, Harper. I knew I had them, but we weren't . . . material."

I smile. "You think I don't know how that feels?" Tate's eyes widen, and he stares at me curiously for a moment.

"I guess you do," he says and gives an abrupt laugh that is

more shock than amusement. "Then that's how it feels? When you . . . dematerialize?"

"More or less." I give a shrug of my own, the baby stirring in my arms then falling asleep again. "I'm still me, but I'm simply not there for a while; then I am again. In the time I am in the darkness, I'm still *me,* but I'm not corporeal. It took me a while to get used to it."

"I don't think I ever could." Tate shudders slightly. "It was not a comfortable sensation. But anyway. I had them, the babies, and I knew I was safe. I could feel my link to Iara, and I could hear you calling to me, Harper. Then suddenly, everything changed." He looks at Iara, who nods and takes up where he leaves off.

"I felt it," she says slowly, frowning in recollection, "before I saw it. Cold. And slippery, like a—a—" She pauses, searching for the word.

"Like a snake," I say quietly.

"Yes! This! Like this." Iara makes a slithering motion with her arm. "I could not see, only feel, but as soon as I feel the touch, the darkness comes. The mist. Cutting me off from Tate, so I cannot feel him. I know only that I have the flowers, that I must stay holding them; but Tate's hand, this I no longer feel, like he is gone from me, from this world."

"He was." Antoine is staring at Tate, his eyes dark with reminiscence. "Your body was still there, but somehow the essence of you wasn't in the pond anymore, Tate. I felt it before I knew it, felt something try to cut the bind between you and me. Then I looked up and just before the mist fell, I realized that even your body seemed to be fading into the mist. Whatever makes you, the essence of you, it was gone."

"Part of me certainly was." Tate glances at Iara. "I could still sense Iara, but I was no longer touching her. I was already in darkness, but until then, it had been a chaotic darkness, turbulent. Suddenly it was deathly still. And I could see her." He looks around at us. "Avery," he says quietly. "Only, she was changed. Not into a wolf, as she said she would. At first, I thought she was a vampire." He frowns. "I still think she's a vampire—but she's something else, too. Something I have never seen before and certainly don't understand. She seemed to shimmer, go in and out of being, changing shape and form. She seemed to spiral through the darkness, almost like smoke." He stops, shaking his head in confusion. "She was both extraordinarily beautiful, like light itself almost, or a rainbow even; then, in the next moment, she was the most terrifying thing I've ever seen, though I honestly don't know how or why." He looks frustrated. "I can't describe it. In that space, she wasn't really a person—more an impression. I *felt* her beauty rather than seeing it. I could see her face, like a mirage, forming, then disappearing again. But what I did know, without any doubt, was that whatever she was had nothing to do with the Avery we know. And she wanted the twins, Harper. She wanted them so badly I could feel it. It was so overwhelming *I* almost—" He chokes on the words, and I try not to shiver at what he isn't saying, at how close we came to losing them all over again.

"It's okay." Antoine leans forward and grips Tate's shoulder briefly, but hard enough to rock the other man away from the sink. "I knew you wouldn't let her take them, Tate. I knew it."

"Only because you called me." Tate meets his eyes openly. "The Maker's summons," he says quietly. "It was the only thing, I think, with the power to call me back, Antoine. Even then, I thought for a moment I wouldn't be able to withstand it. Whatever Avery is now, she's so powerful I had no chance against her. Until Jeremiah called her."

"I heard him." I stare out of the window, where the moon is hovering about the trees. I remember all the nights I have sat here with Avery, in friendship and in times of trouble, watching as the moon rises, and feel a terrible tug of sadness. "I heard Jeremiah call out to her. It seemed to make a difference."

"It was everything." Tate nods. "When he called, her face appeared clearly in the darkness. She was scared, I think. Genuinely confused. For a moment at least, she was entirely herself. And a moment was all it took for your voices to reach into the darkness, to pull us all forward. That, and the babies themselves." He stares at them, wonder and fascination in his eyes. "They knew where to go," he says softly. "They genuinely knew, Harper. It was almost as if they just needed Avery to get out of the way. From there, it was they who carried me." He looks at Antoine. "You were worried they wouldn't know how to come back," he says quietly. "But they knew all along, Antoine. They didn't need me or anyone else, not really. I think that once the portal was open, they knew exactly where and how to travel. Not just along that water path, but along all of them. It was like they had an unerring sense. They tugged me with them. All I did was hang on."

The kitchen is silent for a while, all of us, in our own ways, processing what we've heard. Outside, an owl hoots and an answer comes from deep in the woods. The night outside smells of new growth and soft, fresh flowers. Inside, the kitchen is filled with the wild scents of drying herbs and the comfort of old wood. I nestle into my chair and feel grateful that we are here, together. Safe.

For now.

"What do you think Avery is?" I direct the question to Iara, who takes her time answering.

"This, I do not know. Not truly." She looks around at us. "But whatever she is, she became it with help from the spirit world. She did not use any of us, not Antoine's medicine woman, or Harper's shaman. She worked the magic herself. This is very powerful—and very, very dangerous. It means that in that time, between death and life, she had no protection. Nobody to look over her, to be making certain she is safe as she changes. We do not know what maybe is entering her body at this time. We are not even knowing if she drank a potion, trying to become a wolf. If it was this that killed her, or something else. But we are knowing this: she is now immortal, and she is strong." Iara's face is grave. "Whatever is inside Avery, I am thinking it is from my people. For the snake, that snake inside her—this, I am thinking, is the serpent of the Warao. Or a part of it, at least."

"Keziah?" I look around. "Is that who's inside her?"

Antoine and Cass look at each other, then at Iara, and as one, they all shake their heads. "No." Antoine is definite. "I'm sure it isn't Keziah. I didn't feel her at all."

"Do you think Avery will come back here?" I look around. "Come after the twins?"

"I think we can be sure of it," Antoine says grimly. "But when she does, we'll be ready for her. And she won't get our children, Harper." He puts his hand on my shoulder and I cover it with my own. "I promise you."

My fingers tighten on his hand. "I know, Antoine," I say quietly. "I know."

One by one, the others leave, Tate and Iara to hunt, Connor and Cass for the rooms they keep at the end of the mansion.

"It's strange," I say, trying to keep my voice from wobbling, "being here without Callie and Jeremiah." Gently, I stroke Marguerite's velvet forehead with my thumb. "I wish they could be here."

"I know." Antoine's voice is rough, his hand on my shoulder tightening briefly. "I miss them, too."

We sit there throughout the night, our babies sleeping in our arms, until a pearlescent dawn begins to rise over the slow-moving river.

CHAPTER 23

SHIFTER

It is late afternoon, and Antoine and I are sitting on the grass sloping down to the river beneath a mellow spring sun. The twins are lying on a rug between us, playing with a mobile hanging from a frame Connor made. Because my brother can't help his sense of humor, among the shapes dangling on the mobile are carved wolves.

Hilarious.

"Do they seem bigger than they were yesterday?" I eye Aurelia and Marguerite worriedly. "They don't eat or drink anything except water. I don't understand how they grow so fast."

"And you asked me the same question yesterday." Antoine frowns. "But yes, they do look bigger. Even to someone who knows nothing about babies." He gives me a crooked grin that makes my heart twist with love. "Stronger, too. But we can't really be sure exactly how long they were away." He stops speaking abruptly and shoots me a wary glance. I smile.

"It's okay. They're back now. That's all that matters." The pendants around the twins' necks glow in the sunlight. The fierce, shifting light in their depths has faded in the weeks since they returned to us, but the potency, I know, is still there, dormant. We have no idea when or if the girls will travel again. It took days before Antoine would consent to my bathing them, he was so terrified of what would happen when they went into water. But so far, apart from their complete lack of interest in food, they've been completely normal. *Well*, I think wryly, as Aurelia rolls over entirely unaided and raises her head to look at me with uncanny perception, *more or less normal.*

The reality, of course, is that they aren't normal at all. A few days after they returned, Antoine and I drove to an infant welfare clinic in Jackson. Between us, we compelled the entire staff to examine the twins closely, then to promptly forget us when we left. They told us we had two perfectly healthy babies.

Healthy *six-month-old* babies.

At first, I wanted to weigh and measure them every day. But the growth spurts, we discovered, happen at odd times, with no fixed pattern. For days, they grow exactly like babies should. Then will come a day when they are listless, crying weakly, skin hot and dry and eyes dull. The first couple of times this happened, we all panicked, my deep fears that they can't possibly survive on water alone rising to the surface. But every time, it was water that they craved. And after drinking their own weight in water, a growth spurt happens, literally before our eyes. A month in an hour, or that is how it seems.

Iara discovered, quite by accident, that they like particular flowers or herbs in their water. She left her own cup on the rug underneath a crepe myrtle tree one afternoon as the twins played on the grass, and one of the frilly white flowers fell into the water in it. Marguerite, who usually is the more docile of the two, was close to the cup. Despite having a bottle of her own, she reached toward the cup, crying until Iara held it up to her mouth. Marguerite not only drank thirstily, but then cooed to Aurelia, who also cried until Iara let her drink. After that, on a hunch, we started experimenting with different edible flowers and plants in their water. Some seem to trigger the growth spurts more than others. We haven't yet found a pattern to it, but we have fun mixing up the different plant drinks.

"What's in them today?" Antoine nods at the bottles, eyeing them suspiciously. He has less confidence than I do in our plant concoctions. He never says it aloud, but I know he's terrified that we might be giving the girls some kind of magic potion in every bottle. I, on the other hand, think that we should be trying to find a way to give them whatever magic we can, given they are subsisting on water alone. I can't rid myself of the fear that we are somehow starving them, no matter how much their blooming good health and rapid growth belies the fact.

"White nasturtiums," I say primly. "They seem to like those the most at the moment." Aurelia makes a particularly aggressive roll, and I dart to the end of the blanket and prop her back onto it, my back to the jetty.

"Nasturtiums." Antoine raises his eyebrows. "Isn't it a little early? Never mind," he says hastily, shaking his head. "Stupid question." But the smile he gives me takes any sting out of his words, and in this moment, basking in the late spring sun, the girls playing contentedly, I can almost believe we are a normal family.

Almost.

"Harper." Antoine's voice is low and thrums with warning. "Don't move. Avery is here."

Every nerve in my body tenses. Thunder cracks in the distance, and clouds roll over the sun. An uneasy wind begins to blow.

"There's no need to bring a storm down over my head, Harper. I'm not here to harm you." It is Avery's voice, but it isn't. It's higher and sharper, like metal on glass. I can sense her on the jetty behind me. My eyes are locked on Antoine's, waiting for the smallest signal to sweep the twins up and carry them away. He shakes his head, a tiny, almost-indiscernible gesture that says *no sudden moves.* I grit my teeth. Slowly, keeping the girls blocked between my body and Antoine's, I turn around.

Avery is definitely a vampire.

I knew it already, or at least, we had all suspected it. But Tate was right—she isn't just a vampire. She's something else entirely.

I should be used to transformations by now. I've seen almost everyone I know go through them. But nothing prepares me for Avery's.

Her hair has always been a smooth dark curtain that swished just like a shampoo commercial. Now, though, it has been transformed into a mass of gleaming, snaky curls that seem to move in a kind of optical illusion. It's like her hair is actually alive, writhing about her head, both extraordinarily seductive and equally terrifying. Her eyes are still almond shaped, but now their deep, dark brown has gained a molten gold liquidity, behind which gleams the familiar, shimmering iridescence in aqua and turquoise, like a high mountain lake. "Avery." I crouch, ready to spring forward. "What are you doing here?"

Avery smiles, and it is the most unsettling thing I've ever seen, her face shifting and changing like some kind of watery reflection. "I came to say goodbye to my parents." This time when she smiles, there's a crimson flash of rage and hurt behind the turquoise. "It didn't work out so well."

I shiver involuntarily, my eyes flickering over my shoulder to Antoine.

"What do you mean, it didn't work out so well?" He's standing slightly behind me, facing Avery, his face carefully blank.

"Antoine." Avery's mouth curls in disdain. "I don't need you to clean up after me. I'm more than capable of doing that myself. My parents won't remember I visited them. In fact, they won't remember me at all. They are planning to move to Oklahoma, as it turns out."

"Oklahoma?" I stare at her. "Avery, your parents love it here. And they love you. You can't just make them believe you're dead—"

"But I am dead, Harper. I'm also immortal, but I think you knew that already." She shifts her balance and again, I notice the shimmering quality of her form, as if she isn't truly here at all, but is a fluid, incorporeal shape.

"What are you, Avery?" Antoine's voice is calm and direct. "And why did you try to take our children in the water paths?"

"Ah." Avery gives another unsettling smile. "Those answers are not simple. I will answer the second question first: I did not intend to find myself in the water paths. All I wanted, when I took your blood, Harper, was to use it to change myself into a wolf. I had the ingredients you used, even the jar that Connor drank from, with traces left inside. Yes," she says, watching me, "that's how long I've been thinking of this. Didn't you ever wonder, Harper, what it was like, being Natchez? Being a direct descendant of the folks that your people colonized and murdered? To have access to centuries of genetic memory and spirit knowledge—yet not be able to *use* it in any real way? Everything my people once were has been destroyed. And yet what have we all done these past few years, Harper, other than sacrifice ourselves to keep you and Antoine safe?" She takes a step forward, the air around her shimmering. "Tate, Cass, and I are the real holders of the magic in this place by birthright. But in the end, we gave everything to ensure that you and Antoine— and now your twins—are safe. Hasn't that ever bothered you?"

"Yes, it's bothered me," I say quietly, holding her eyes. "You know it has, Avery." Her eyes flash dangerously, and I feel an answering rush of savagery. Behind her, the river begins to ripple uneasily.

"This isn't helping." Antoine cuts brutally across our conversation. "You said you didn't intend to find yourself in the water paths. That you planned to become a wolf."

"Yes." Avery's eyes shift to him. "I had help, a spirit voice I had accessed. A woman. She knew the magic I needed. We agreed she would help me."

Antoine's eyes narrow. "In exchange for what?"

Avery laughs, a rippling, unsettling sound that disturbs the air around her. "You know more than you like to admit, Antoine, don't you? Yes, there was an exchange. I would have to become something more than just wolf. Something that was both vampire and wolf. It was dangerous, she warned me; but it would also make me more powerful than either wolf or vampire. More powerful than anyone, or anything, in existence." Her eyes gleam, and I can see how this would have appealed to Avery, who has always resented being unable to use what powers she had, has always wanted to be *more*.

"Who was this spirit?" I ask. "Was it Keziah?"

"Oh, no." Avery shakes the snaky mass of curls. It is one of the most disturbing things I've ever seen, like a mass of serpents writhing about her face. "Keziah is definitely gone. No, this is another spirit altogether, though I can't say her name to you. She did warn me the transformation would be dangerous. I went high up into the Appalachian Mountains to perform the magic. Right into a cave behind a mountain waterfall. I don't think anyone had been there in centuries."

I have a sudden flash of memory: the cave, back in Haiti, where I had found the statue of Abatey. I feel a ripple of unease down my spine.

"I didn't realize, though, that the magic would take me into the water paths." For a moment her face falters, and there is a glimpse of the old Avery amid the uncanny, shifting colors. "That's what I came to tell you, Harper. I never meant to enter them, or to try to take your children. I don't like you. I'll admit it. But I had no intention of trying to hurt you like that. It was after I—died. I was—lost for a while."

I nod. I know that feeling well; I think all of us who have traveled this path do.

"During that time, it was all the spirit. She was the one who had control—until I was given the blood. Your blood, Harper."

We are both staring at her, but it's Antoine who speaks first and asks the question for both of us. "Who gave you the blood, Avery? Who else was there?"

"It was a wolf." The unsettling smile is back. "One of the Appalachian pack. The daughter of an alpha. Someone I'd already met."

"Bailey." I say the name with certainty; I know I'm right. "The girl who came and told Remy and the pack about the dreams, the Mating."

"Exactly." Avery's smile has turned into a predatory snarl. "The spirit came to Bailey in a dream, promised her a new mate if she did what she was asked. Bailey came to the cave and found me on the ground. She gave me the blood."

"And then you took her." Fascination and revulsion war in Antoine's eyes. "Bailey was your first kill. You took the wolf inside you."

"You couldn't have done it," Avery says, her eyes flashing. "Or you, Harper. Maybe nobody could have survived taking a wolf as their first kill, other than me. But I had the spirit to work the magic I needed to become what I am, to survive it."

"And what are you, exactly?" Antoine asks.

"I don't know what you would call it. Remy—" A fierce light stabs the air in front of her eyes. "Remy called me a Shifter."

"A Shifter." I glance at Antoine. "Have you heard that term before?"

Antoine shakes his head slowly, still watching her. "Not in any real context, no. Once, perhaps, centuries ago." His eyes cut to me. "During the period I met El Viajero," he says quietly. We stare at each other for a moment, trying to work through the implications of this, but I know now isn't the time. I force myself to look back at Avery. "You said that Remy saw you?"

Avery looks away. Her long, slender form, far more willowy than it was even before this, ripples and wavers, lit by the golden sunlight from beyond my rain squall, making her seem almost translucent. "He found me just after I took the wolf." Her voice is quiet, and in it I can still sense the old, hurt Avery. "Unfortunately, it seems that the wolf packs hate Shifters even more than humans do." She turns back, her eyes and voice once more as brittle as cut glass. "All this, all the danger, and still, it seems, I'm not enough for Remy."

I go to speak but she waves me away impatiently. "I didn't come here for friendship, Harper. My time here is over, and I'm planning to get as far away as I can. Leave this side of the world completely, for a while anyway. There's nothing for me here. Not now. I just came to reassure you that your children are safe. From me, at least." She frowns slightly. "I didn't know that the spirit wanted your children. That's what I came to say to you. I don't know why I was sent into those water paths. I can't travel them again. I've tried. I can't even sense them. Whatever it was that took me there, it wasn't me, and it won't happen again."

She looks between Antoine and me. "I don't like you, Harper. And I don't want to be part of whatever strange little supernatural party you all have going on here. I know Jem is gone, and he was the only one of you I was ever truly friends with. Remy is gone," she says bitterly. "There's nothing left for me here. And if I don't belong with the wolves, and I don't belong with the vampires, then I need to find a place of my own. Maybe even a people of my own." Her eyes drop to the twins, then come back up to look at us. "Don't try to find me," she says quietly. "You won't. And don't expect to ever see me again. But you have my word on this, if it helps: I won't ever harm you or your children. You have my promise, Harper."

She holds my eyes for long enough to see the relief spread

through mine. The sun breaks through the clouds overhead, and Avery looks up at it and smiles, a twisted, humorless curve of her mouth that is as unsettling as it is ephemeral.

"Good luck, Avery," I say quietly. "Wherever you go, whatever you do—I hope you are happy. I truly do."

"Happy." The brittle laugh cuts the air again. "I wonder why everyone works so hard to be happy. And all you get is a moment in time. It never lasts." She tilts her head impatiently. "Anyway. There's only one last thing." She meets my eyes, then Antoine's. "If Remy comes here," she says quietly, "you can tell him I'm gone. Tell him I'll never disturb his peace again." Her eyes fill with a sad resolve. "Not ever," she whispers. She nods at me. "Goodbye, Harper."

"Goodbye, Avery."

But I'm talking to the air, for Avery is gone, only a faint ripple on the wind any indication that she was there at all.

CHAPTER 24

FIVE YEARS LATER

The kitchen inside the mansion is still and peaceful, but outside, the sounds of shrieking children pierce the afternoon heat. I feel a soft rush of air behind me and smile. "Tired of the other parents already?"

"You can't talk. Don't think I didn't notice you sneak off, pretending you had cooking to do. As if you haven't already made enough to feed an army." Antoine's arms snake around my waist, and he kisses my neck slowly enough to make me shiver. "But yes," he murmurs against my skin. "I definitely prefer it when it's just the two of us."

"It will be, soon enough." I turn in his arms.

"Are you having second thoughts?" Drawing me close, he kisses me, so long and sweet that I could almost forget about the chaos of the twins' birthday party in full swing on our lawn. "You know we can stay, if you want." His whisper is husky against my ear. His lips brush my temple. I shake my head gently against them.

"It's odd enough that our five-year-old twins look more like third graders. Let alone that their father does some mysterious work online that nobody understands. Or that their mother has a best-selling nursery that produces flowers in the middle of winter. And that's before we get into the fact that neither of us has aged a day—or the twins' odd eating habits."

"They do a good job of pretending." Antoine grins. "Aurelia actually made an entire hot dog disappear a few moments ago. It was nothing if not impressive."

I groan. "Please tell me she wasn't torturing Billy Mason. I had to bribe his mother with almost an entire garden bed of seedlings after the last time they got into it."

"Last I looked, the kids were all happily taking part in Cass's treasure hunt. Iara had all the mothers begging for her jambalaya recipe, Tate was distracting the snobbiest of the Karens with historical anecdotes, and Connor was introducing the men to his home brew. I think we're good for now." His hand strokes my back, and despite his levity, his eyes on mine are watchful. "But I meant what I said. It isn't too late to change your mind, Harper. I know you want the girls to have as normal an upbringing as they can."

I smile, but I'm already shaking my head. "It isn't just us. Cass and Connor are leaving, too."

Antoine frowns. "They are?"

I nod, smiling. Now feels like the right time to tell him. "You know Cass said she was finally ready to study music? Well, she's been accepted to the University of Granada! How could she not go? Connor told me he found a house there, in Spain, to renovate. It's a medieval mansion dating back to the Moorish occupation, so he's in seventh heaven."

"Spain!" Antoine shakes his head, smiling. "Perfect."

"I thought so, since we were planning to spend the next years in England, France and Spain. Tate and Iara already spend most of the year traveling. And it won't do the girls any harm to learn other languages, live in other countries. This will always be their home." My smile falters and Antoine brushes the hair away from my face.

"They're healthy," he says quietly. We've had this conversation so many times that I already know what he's going to say, just as he knows it doesn't help. "Just because Tessa said she never saw them older than their midtwenties means nothing. She also said you shouldn't worry, and that it will all make sense eventually."

"But what if that's just what they told her to tell us? We already know they keep secrets." I glance at the old musket mounted high on the wall—out of the reach of tiny hands. At the age of two, during Connor's renovation of this room, Aurelia had taken hold of the musket and abruptly disappeared, taking Marguerite with her. When the two eventually returned, they were dressed in different clothing and covered in dirt, pale, listless, and desperately thirsty—and at least a month older than when they'd left. That was the first time we worked out what lies behind their sudden growth spurts, as well as the uncomfortable fact that the twins don't need water to travel. Since then, we've done all we can to keep them separated from objects that may lead to dangerous places in history. With two family members who have been alive for three centuries, that has proven challenging. Fortunately, it seems that the twins can only travel together, or at least, neither seems inclined to try it alone. We, of course, would prefer they don't travel at all. But it's a little hard to monitor when they also have the ability to return to the same moment they left. And the older they get, the more clever they become. We both get cold shudders when we imagine what might happen when they hit teenage years; the terrible twos were more than enough to turn even vamp hair gray, if that were possible.

But beyond our fears about the time they may be spending in the water paths, among people and places we can't possibly know, is the overriding terror that they never grow any older than their midtwenties. No matter what Tessa told me, I can't rid myself of the gnawing, terrible fear that we simply lose the girls forever at that age. I try not to think of it. I try to treasure every moment we have. But those years are going by awfully fast, particularly given the twins' rapid—or time-defying—rate of growth.

"We've agreed not to dwell on this too much." Antoine holds my face in his hands. "We already know they don't need human food. Their bodies simply don't function normally. When they get a cut, it heals almost as fast as ours do. Even Marguerite's broken arm—"

"I know, I know." I nod impatiently. That, of all the things that have happened so far, was our biggest indication that the girls truly might be immortal. Marguerite fell while climbing a tree when she was four, an endeavor undoubtedly suggested by Aurelia, who has yet to come across a challenge she doesn't want to throw herself at. Marguerite's arm was broken in three places. Despite the ability we have to repair anything with our blood, Antoine and I decided to take her to a hospital. Okay, I decided to take her to a hospital. I guess a part of me thought it was another one of those human experiences she should have.

Only, by the time we'd actually pulled into the parking lot, Marguerite was happily waving her drink bottle around with the injured arm. Which was, by then, completely healed.

The twins don't get sick. Ever. Their teeth appeared overnight, without so much as a cry to herald their arrival. And more than once, they've picked up something sharp or hot and barely even winced. Their athletic ability is far more developed than their age; we had to take them out of judo class when the infamous Billy Mason sustained a particularly nasty black eye.

No matter how I might want to seize on all these things and try to see them as evidence that the girls will live longer than the age that seems to be approaching all too quickly, the truth is that I can't know what will happen. All I can do is live one extraordinary day at a time—and hope.

All of these things are reasons to move. And to keep moving.

I have a feeling we won't be able to stay in one place for long. And for someone who always dreamed of a home that I could stay in forever, that my children would know is their home, that has been hard.

"We'll be fine." I force a smile and wave Antoine away. "You go. I'll be out in a moment. I just want to do a few things." I wave my hand in the air and Antoine, who knows my fancies well enough, smiles gently. Touching my face, he turns and leaves, and I can't help but grin when I see Billy Mason's father, Ray, bustle importantly toward him as soon as he spies Antoine on the porch. Ray is a joiner. He's been hoping Antoine will join his charitable organization for years and never misses a chance to press him. Antoine is of the opinion that his wallet is a far better team player than he himself and has learned to preempt any social gathering by sending a particularly generous dona- tion before it. "Ray," I hear Antoine say resignedly. "I hope you got my check last week?"

They move off down the lawn, and the mansion falls rela- tively silent again. On an impulse, I walk through to the library.

The mural on the wall is long finished. In the early days after the twins came home, I was too scared to sleep much, in case I woke to find them gone again. I painted every night. The mural wound up even more magical than I could have envisaged, exactly like a picture into the past. I painted all our faces into the image, though carefully disguised, so that it would only be obvious on closer inspection. Despite the mural being a period piece, I couldn't bear to portray Cass as a slave, so I painted her and Connor reclining beneath a tree, hidden from the crowd, capturing the particular mix of gentleness and strength I always see in her. Antoine, of course, I made the plantation owner, joking with Tate, dressed as a trapper, who is in turn eyeing Iara, standing nearby. And Tessa, my beautiful sister, walks arm in arm with me by the river.

I even painted Avery, for no matter how utterly she is gone, she is part of our story and still will be, I feel. We are immortal, after all. There are many years in which our paths might cross. Avery is walking alone on the porch, willowy and beautiful, staring out at the crowd. Her story, I know, is still untold.

I walk past the mural, touching it lightly, and press on the button. The bookshelf, loaded now with all the books Connor, Tessa, and I always loved, those Antoine and Tate have collected, and the twins' baby books, swings silently open. Taking a deep breath, I walk slowly down the stairs.

The stench of charred, dead fire has gone. All trace of Keziah, it seems, has left the earth here. The stairs smell musty and old, but I detect no trace of danger. I reach the door at the bottom. It is closed; regardless if Keziah is gone or not, it seems wrong to leave that heavy iron door open. Now, however, I turn the big handle, and the iron bolts slide easily aside. Supernatural strength has its benefits.

The cellar, of course, is empty. The coffins that once held Keziah and Caleb are long gone. The old wooden shelves are neatly swept and clean, but bare. We don't store anything down here. But today, now that I'm leaving at last, I want to see it, to remember how it all began. And perhaps, to remind myself of all we have overcome.

We beat that curse. I stand in the place where Keziah and Caleb slept for centuries. A curse nobody thought would ever be broken was defeated. Not by strength or cunning, but by love. Everything we have overcome has been done with love.

I breathe in the still, quiet air. I'm not sure what I expect—a whisper, an echo, perhaps. Some kind of finality.

But nothing comes, and after a while, I close the door behind me and walk upstairs.

When I come out into the library, the afternoon sunlight is streaming in through the French windows, turning the floorboards butter yellow, and my brother is standing in front of the mural. He raises an arm in acknowledgment of my presence as I emerge from the stairwell but doesn't turn around.

"Connor." I come to stand beside him. "I thought you were entertaining the fathers."

"I thought I'd let Antoine have the pleasure." He shoots me a wicked grin. "It's his final chance. I figured he should enjoy it."

"You're evil."

"I do my best."

We look at the mural together for a while, the sounds of childish laughter drifting through the window. "You know," Connor says quietly, "I was standing here, while you were down in the cellar, thinking that this was what I always imagined. This day." His eyes flicker to me then away again. "Children, running on the lawn, playing in the trees. You and me, happy. Laughing with each other. It's all I ever hoped for. All I dreamed of." He shrugs self-consciously. "And now, here it is."

"But is it, Connor? Truly?" I turn to him, scrutinizing his face, trying and failing to sense what he feels. Of all the things I can read, Connor has never really been one of them. Maybe it's my blood in his veins, or maybe it's just family dynamics, but Connor's true heart is known to Cass alone. The rest of us see only the face he shows us.

He laughs softly and faces me. "Yes, Harper. It is. Truly." He nods outside, and I turn to see Cass running through the tall grass by my water garden, laughing as the children chase her, shrieking delightedly. "I never imagined a future with someone like Cass," he says softly, his eyes resting on her long, lithe figure. "I never even began to imagine I could win someone like her. Not for a day, let alone an eternity. And this house." He gestures around at it. "I didn't just restore it. We brought it back to life, Harper. All of us. The Marigny mansion is now a monument on the historical trail, a landmark. Heck, even the governor came for the official opening." He shoots me a grin that I return. It had been a guilty pleasure, I admit, to watch all of Mississippi society fall all over themselves to win an invitation to the ball we held to celebrate the end of the restoration. There are many things, I imagine, that a long life teaches a person, and how to hold a rocking party, it turns out, is one of them. There's a picture displayed in the salon of Antoine, Tate, Connor, and the governor, all resplendent in tuxedos, smiling for the media. The photo made the front page of the state papers, something that made Antoine roll his eyes and mutter darkly about the dangers posed to immortals by cameras and digital research.

"And now," Connor continues, "I have more than enough money to branch out and start new projects. Like this one in Spain." He nods slowly. "I thought, when we came here, that I wanted a forever home. A place where I could sit on the porch in a rocking chair and play with your kids." He turns and meets my eyes, and for once there is no caution in his eyes, just openness. "But that was before I understood that forever is a very long time. And that your children will be with us for it all. Eternity is liberating, Harper." He gives me a crooked smile. "It means there is time to do all I ever dreamed of, and more. And most importantly, that the people I love most in the world will be there to share it with me."

"That makes me happier than you could possibly know." I give him a watery smile. Outside, a sudden gust of wind turns the leaves over, and the guests look around, startled. For once, I don't try to control it.

"I know what you aren't saying." Connor steps forward and touches my arm. "I know you're scared the twins won't be here to see that eternity."

Clouds join the wind now, and the guests start gathering their belongings, casting uneasy looks at the sky.

"I think they will. In fact, Harper, I'm sure of it."

I frown, searching his face. "You can't be sure. None of us can."

Connor gives me one of his old, crooked grins, full of mischief and wry humor. "I think we can," he says quietly. "Why did you just go down into that cellar? To remind yourself of how far we've come, all of us. None of this happened by chance. You, me, Antoine, Cass. Jeremiah and Callie, Tate and Iara—even Avery. We found Tessa again, Harper." He shakes his head. "If that isn't a miracle, then I don't know what is. You and Antoine made me a wolf—an immortal wolf. Antoine brought an entire pack of wolves back to life and gave them immortality. Cass is a vampire, Avery a Shifter, whatever that is." He casts his eyes skyward with a droll expression. "Shamans, ancient deities, nature magic—and somehow, amid all that chaos, you and Antoine had twin girls who can time travel." He shakes his head and looks at me, a curious curl to his mouth. "After all that, if you don't believe in miracles, or in your own ability to overcome any obstacle in your path, then you haven't been living the same life I have." Coming closer, he puts his arm around my shoulders, pulling me roughly against his side as the first raindrops spatter against the window and the guests begin tumbling in through the back door.

"I have no idea what the rest of forever looks like for us," Connor says. "But we'll face it like we always have, Harper. Together. And no matter what it throws at us, we will find a way through it." He pulls back and looks at me. "Deal?"

I laugh softly and touch my forehead to his shoulder. "Deal."

The peace of the library is shattered by Antoine's head at the door, his expression one of exasperation. "Harper." He nods impatiently at Connor. "You need to get out here. One more inane conversation and I might end up eating parent for dinner. Also," he glances around, "I think the twins have—gone."

"Gone?" I stare at him. "That's the *second* thing you had to say?" I'm already heading through the French windows toward the water garden, where I last saw them playing. As I move to the water's edge Antoine is behind me saying resignedly, "But

I'm pretty sure I know where they've gone." Just as I am about to ask what he means, Aurelia and Marguerite materialize before us on the edge of the water garden. Their matching fairy costumes are dripping wet, and they are both giggling conspiratorially.

Fairy costumes.

I fix them with a grim eye. "You two," I say sternly. "Where did you just go?" Antoine comes to stand beside me, his arms folded. He's doing his best to look forbidding, but Aurelia, who can wrap her father around one tiny pinkie with no effort at all, turns to him instead of me to answer. "Even you said the party was boring," she points out with the unflinching honesty of childhood. "And Billy started crying. So Margy an' me went to see Auntie Tessa. And it was fun," she says defiantly, slipping her hand into her twin's. Marguerite looks up at me guiltily. "We played hide and seek."

I'm fighting hard not to laugh.

"We saw you, Momma," Marguerite says softly. "But we stayed out of sight, so you didn't see us." She looks at me curiously. "You were little. Like us."

I remember that long-ago day, Tessa trying to tell me about the new friends she had met and played with, and how I didn't believe her. Unexpected tears catch in my throat. I kneel, holding out my arms, and my babies run into them. I pull them close. "How was she?" I whisper into their hair, inhaling their sweet, babyish scent. "How was your Auntie Tessa?"

"She was good. She told us a story," says Aurelia, her hand curled into my neck.

"Did she, now?"

"Yes. And she said . . ." They chatter on, and I look over their heads at Antoine.

"You know," he says quietly as the girls fall silent, "I'm pretty sure Tate can make up some excuse for us."

"What are you thinking?" I ask. "We haven't even cut the cake yet."

Antoine raises his eyebrows and kneels down. "Girls," he says gravely. "Would you rather cut the cake? Or go to the fairy place in the woods and get Momma to make you a rainbow?"

I tilt my head at him. *Not fair.* His grin is even more wicked than Connor's.

"Fairy place! Fairy place!" The girls are jumping up and down, their silvery fabric wings dancing in the sunlight that's poking through the rainclouds. I glance guiltily up the hill, where Tate is standing on the porch watching us. He's also clearly listening in, because he waves his arms and says, "A family emergency it is, then. You owe me one, brother."

Antoine grins, then turns to me. "Shall we?"

I shake my head. "You're impossible."

And then we're running, our girls in our arms, through the wild forest, to the clearing in the woods where Antoine once dreamed of building a life. The spot our beautiful girls call the Fairy Place. The air smells fresh-washed and new after my rain, and the autumn breeze carries the scent of the forest, pine-clean and intoxicating.

Overhead, a multicolored rainbow bursts into life, arcing across the sky like hope.

CHAPTER 25

PARIS, TEN YEARS LATER

Dearest Harper,

It is the day after you visited for the last time. I think I will be gone very soon. I saw it in your face; I feel it in my body. I don't think I will ever know if you find this letter or not. I slipped it into Marguerite's jacket pocket today when she and Aurelia went to fetch me some water. She was wearing a black wool jacket that looked very chic. She told me she bought it in Paris and intended to give it to you because you admired it so much.

I'm breaking rules by writing this. But I think—I hope—I have found a loophole. Things cannot exist in two places. But very soon, I will not exist, and so I think the timelines can't be blurred by what I am about to tell you.

I know this letter will likely prompt a thousand more questions that I can't answer even if I wanted to. The twins each have their own stories. Their own stories to live, to tell in their own time and their own words. Nothing I can do or write will alter the water paths they travel, or change the joy and pain you find in being their mother. You and Antoine are the supernatural parents of two extraordinary, magical girls, destined to live extraordinary, magical lives. There's nothing predictable about that.

If someone had told you, before you moved to the mansion and met Antoine, all that lay ahead—would you have chosen it? Would you have moved into a house that you knew had monsters in the cellar and a vampire owner? I think you probably would have run. Far away. And yet, every turn of this story has led you farther down that magical pathway, to a world richer than you could have ever imagined. I hope that for you, motherhood is just another part of that pathway, one that gets richer with every year.

If I know you, Harper, I know that you will be living in a constant state of terror, wondering if your twins will be taken from you, like so much else has. I know you're afraid because I told you I've never seen the girls aged past their midtwenties. What I do know is this: while your girls age faster than human children, they are magical, not human. And there comes a time when they stop aging altogether. I don't know if they are immortal like you (I will never even get used to that word, let alone writing it as if it's fact), because the water paths forbid the girls from telling me too much of their stories.

You can't protect the twins from what they'll encounter on the paths they will travel, nor alter their course. You can only be the bank on either side that holds them, for as long as you can. You must simply love them. And have faith that, in time, they will face their own battles with the same courage you've always had.

After all, isn't that what a life is? Love, faith, and the courage to stand and face the battles we must?

Know that now, as I face the final battle on my own path,

I am with you, Harper, as you are with me.

ALWAYS.

Tessa

~

Thankyou for travelling the water paths this far. There is still much more to come in the Nightgarden universe.

Jeremiah and Callie's story continues in Fleur-de-Lis, a sample of which is on the following pages. Avery's story continues in an ongoing serial, The Wolves of Bayou Lune, with an excerpt also on the following pages.

The Waterpaths saga, which follows on from this series, is already scheduled for release. Follow me on Patreon for updates and excerpts at https://www.patreon.com/Fehupress and read on for samples!

FLEUR-DE-LIS SAMPLE

PROLOGUE

Paris, 20th October, 1793.

Claude Duval was accustomed to unexpected guests arriving at odd hours. The sign outside his small Paris shop read *coutelier,* and all knew Paris had many fine cooks who required their knives to be sharpened. Sometimes such visitors came hurriedly, late at night, for who could tell when the capricious masters of La Révolution may require a particularly complex dish? A close observer may have noticed that on occasion, three might enter, and only two return; or, as had been the case tonight, two enter, and three leave. But his was a busy little shop, and people in Paris knew one another, after all. There was little about a small coutelier to rouse the suspicions of the Garde Nationale. Particularly when Monsieur Duval's shop was located in an alley parallel to Rue Vivienne, where some of Paris's finest courtesans could be found inside their Maison Closes. These establishments, and the ladies within, were of far more interest to the guards than a portly little knifemaker. No, there was little to remark upon about Monsieur Duval's unassuming shop front, particularly late on a chill September

evening, when a steady rain had kept all but the most determined off the streets, and even the Maison Closes had begun to
dim their red lanterns.

So when a soft knock came upon his door, Monsieur Duval
had already retired with a brandy of rather fine quality, and was
about to exchange his trousers for a nightshirt. At first he
thought the timid knock downstairs was intended for someone
else. However, accustomed as he was to unusual visitors, he
stiffened, listening closely.

"Mon dieu." The soft knock was unmistakable this time.
Monsieur Duval, moved hastily to the stairs. Guidry had left
with the French Count some hours ago. Unless something had
gone badly wrong, he should not return here tonight. And if
something had gone badly wrong, Monsieur Duval thought
darkly, Guidry should know better than to lead the trouble to
his door.

Thus it was with some trepidation that he put his eye to the
crack between door and wall. There was a girl on the doorstep,
carrying a large parcel. Trying to discern what it was, Monsieur
Duval pushed his face so hard into the wood that a splinter bit
his cheek. He gave an involuntary yelp of surprise. The girl
looked sharply at the crack, and, though she couldn't have
known it, right into his eyes. Leaning close, she whispered:
"Boucher."

Monsieur Duval froze. For a moment, he truly debated
pretending he was not there. He thought longingly of his very
good brandy, and the peaceful night's sleep he had been looking
forward to. Then he thought of Guidry's gleaming topaz eyes,
and rather unsettling teeth; and, more to the point, the rather
large sum of money Guidry owed him after last night's raucous
game of dice. Cursing under his breath, he opened the door.

"Viens, viens," he said irritably, ushering the girl inside. "Allors
—and you are English. Of course you are," he said, shifting
languages with even less enthusiasm as he shut the door. "No

French woman would wear her hair like this, *non—*" Then he turned back, and got his first full look at the strange creature before him. His mouth opened in a perfect O of surprise, and he took a step backwards, unsure what, exactly, had just walked through his door.

It was not a parcel the girl was carrying. It was a bundle. Or, rather, it was two bundles. Two tightly swaddled, very small, very *alive* bundles.

"*Non, non,*" he said, backing away, waving his hands defensively in front of him. "This, I will not have. Guidry and his women! I do not know how you come to know this name, Boucher; no, I do not. But this time, Guidry, he takes a step too far. *Oui,* I am French, and so of course for *moralité,* you understand, I do not care; Guidry may take every woman of Rue Vivienne as he might choose. But now this, to send me his *bâtards;* this, it is insupportable! *Tiens!* And you, *cherie,* you must leave my shop immediately."

Chest huffing with indignation, he was already reaching for the door when the girl spoke.

"*Sil vous plait, Monsieur Duval. Ces enfants ne sont pas de Guidry. Se ne sont pas les miens. Mais ils ont besoin de votre aide. Et moi aussi.*" Please, Monsieur Duval. These children are not Guidry's, nor mine. But they need your help. As do I.

Her accent, Monsieur Duval noticed grudgingly, was not terrible, though French was clearly her second language. Her tongue held an odd inflection that was not unlike Guidry's own. And her clothes! Monsieur Duval stared at her closely, noticing her strange garb properly for the first time. Men's trousers were not unheard of for revolutionary women, but he'd never seen anything like these olive green things— with outside pockets, no less!— and her shirt was no more than a cotton undergarment. As for her shoes —well, they certainly weren't made of leather, and were quite the oddest colour, with a strange slash embroidered on the side. He couldn't help wonder if the slash was some kind of code.

He sighed. So many secrets, these days.

"Well." He pursed his lips. "I suppose you must come inside, then. But I make no promises, you understand. And Guidry, he will pay much coin for this, yes!" Shaking his head and muttering to himself about arrogant revolutionaries who thought nothing of others, he led the newcomer into the small kitchen at the rear of the shop. Hidden in the pantry was a staircase that led to a downstairs cellar, which in turn led to a passageway that came out in a particular Maison Close by the name of La Rose. It's existence was a carefully guarded secret, one known only to a select number of people. Each of those people had a password known only to them. One they did not share, with anyone.

Boucher belonged to Guidry de Anhoia. Why it was being used by an oddly dressed child carrying two newborn babies, late on a rainy Paris night, was a complete mystery.

But Monsieur Duval was certain of one thing: it was a mystery that likely meant trouble. And despite his unorthodox connections, or perhaps because of them, trouble was something Monsieur Duval tried very hard to avoid.

Seating himself on one side of the wooden table, he gestured to the stool on the other. Surreptitiously he pushed his brandy to one side—some things were sacred, and good brandy, in his opinion, was one of them—and instead poured them both a cup of the raw red table wine favored under the new regime. The girl stared at the cup with an oddly blank expression. Duval had seen such hollow eyed shock before, and for the first time since the unusual stranger had arrived, he felt an unwelcome twinge of pity. Mentally cursing his own weakness, he pushed aside the terrible wine, reached for the brandy and pushed it toward her. "Drink, child," he said gently. "It will help, I think."

Slowly the girl shook her head. "It won't," she said, in an

empty, dead tone. "It ain' never helped no-one before as I've ever seen. Don' see why it would now."

"Of course it will help. It comes from the south, and is quite the best brandy in Paris, *ma petit*." Monsieur Duval eyed her curiously. "There is nothing in this world that this brandy, she cannot help, *n'est ce pas?*"

The girl's mouth twitched at the corners. "Well," she murmured. "I guess it ain't like anyone from Social is watchin'." Raising the glass with a wary look, she sipped it, winced, and put the glass back down. "I don' suppose you got any water?"

"Water? In Paris?" Monsieur Duval shuddered. "Drink the brandy, child. It is much safer." He was about to ask what on earth *Social* was, when on cue, one of the two small bundles, who had hitherto remained silent, began to cry in a high, thin wail. Monsieur Duval, who knew less about infants than he did young women dressed in strange clothes, eyed it suspiciously.

"Does it need feeding?" he asked, much as one might ask if a rabid dog needed water.

The young girl looked at him. To Monsieur Duval's absolute horror, her eyes filled with tears. "I don't know," she whispered. "I don't know what they need." Seeing his discomfort, she gulped a much larger swallow of the brandy. When she took her hand away from the glass, Monsieur Duval noticed that her fingers left behind bloody prints. Staring at them, the girl paled even further, slowly raising her eyes to Monsieur Duval.

Giving up all hope of a peaceful evening, the coutelier reached behind the curtain for the bottle of brandy, and poured himself a large glass. "I think," he said quietly, "that you had better start at the beginning, and tell me everything."

The girl closed her eyes. When she opened them again they were clearer, but also detached, as if she had gone somewhere inside herself.

"I was standing in the bedroom," she began, "holding the twins, who had just been born."

FLEUR-DE-LIS CHAPTER 1

CALLIE'S STORY

Mississippi, Modern Day

"Your babies," Callie whispered, clutching the two small bodies close to her chest. "Your miracles, Harper."

Tears blurred her eyes. Not an hour ago, she had sworn to protect the babies she now held. But the creature staring back at her was no longer the Harper who had given birth to them. This Harper bore no resemblance to the gentle friend Callie had met two years ago when she arrived in Deepwater with a backpack and nowhere else to go.

This Harper was a newborn vampire, with gleaming eyes and a face of exquisite, detached perfection.

Harper moved forward, and Callie shrank back, holding the twins close, fear clutching at her throat. She was no match for Harper. No human ever could be.

Just as Callie braced for attack, Harper paused. Something, a strange flash of recognition, lit the strange indigo and bronze eyes. She opened her mouth and the voice that emerged was weak and shaken, but still the voice of the girl who had, until only moments ago, been Callie's friend, and the only true family she had ever known.

"Go." Harper's voice was a frail rasp. Callie knew that this moment of emotion was fleeting, a last shadow of the human inside Harper's new vampiric form. "Take my children, Callie, and go!"

Go where? Callie froze, terrified and uncertain. Harper and Keziah were just beyond the open windows. At the door, Tate and Jeremiah were fighting the newborn vampires threatening Callie and the twins. Callie's heart caught as Jeremiah spun just in time to avoid a deathly lunge. She had to help him.

He can't die! Suddenly all the things she had been too cowardly to say rose in Callie's throat; but before she could give them voice, Guidry, waking from his injuries in human form now instead of wolf, leaped to his feet to face her, blocking her line of sight.

"Rue Vivienne!" he roared, his eyes blazing as they alighted on the bloodied knife in her hand, the knife he had so recently gifted her. "Remember, Callie!"

And abruptly, like the pieces of a jigsaw fitting into place, Callie knew exactly what to do.

If we stay here, the twins will die.

Even so, for a split second she hesitated, her eyes searching for the one person in the room that mattered more to her than any other. Jeremiah was turning away from the fight at the door, his face stricken with horror. "Callie!" He started across the room toward her, but Callie knew he could not make it in time. "No!"

In what felt like slow motion, Callie's eyes swiveled back to Harper. Tears were rolling down the perfect, preternatural features. "Go," Harper whispered, black clouds of grief and terror across the shimmering light of her new eyes. "Go, and be safe." She was not speaking to Callie. Her words were for the twins to whom she had so recently given birth. They must have heard their mother despite her changed form, and understood her meaning, for two small fists reached out to touch the hilt of the bloodied knife in Callie's hand. Harper tore a necklace from her neck and threw it with preternatural accuracy through the window, where it landed on the hilt of the knife. Callie's fingers closed over the blood filled vial hanging from the silver chain.

Callie stared at Jeremiah, fixing his ashen face in her mind, his serious blue eyes deep into her soul.

She closed her hand around the tiny fists on the hilt of the knife, and felt Harper's vial in her hand pulse with an odd strength, as if it were pulling her forward. "Goodbye," she whispered; but already a strange darkness had fallen all around, and she didn't know if Jeremiah heard the word or not.

Callie felt as if she was falling. The darkness was like being caught in a torrent of black water, conflicting currents battering her body with bruising force. Her only thought was that she could not, she must not, let go of the babies. Her only point of awareness was the pulsating weight of the pendant in her fingers and the hilt of the knife they all three held. Even in the darkness and confusion Callie could feel their three distinct hands. She even knew which belonged to whom, and in the seemingly endless confusion, she knew each twin in some intimate, indelible way. One, the twin Callie saw born first, burned hot, her little fist gripping the hilt with a fierce, almost angry, strength. The second born infant barely touched the knife, her tiny hand frail and cool, as if she was taken by the knife rather than directing it. Different though they might have been, when they cried it was together, a sudden, sharp cry of loss amid the dark chaos that both hurt and frightened Callie; then they fell silent, which frightened her even more. The tumbling chaos smoothed into a dark, indigo sea. Callie realized she was no longer falling, and that the light had changed.

She opened her eyes.

She was lying on something damp that felt smooth and hard under her face, and smelled pungent, of human and animal waste and something else, a sharp, metallic scent that some unscrambled part of Callie's mind associated with danger. It was night time. Lamps atop curiously elegant wrought iron posts burned a dull, flickering yellow. In the distance she could hear a rhythmic, hollow rapping. Overwhelming all other senses, though, was a sharp, desperate need for water. Callie felt as parched as if she had been wandering in the desert.

She scrambled to her feet, pulling the babies close to her chest. The twins stared up at her with wide, solemn blue eyes. *Is it my imagination,* Callie thought, *or do their eyes hold a a darker shadow than before, an odd awareness of loss?* Their skin, too, seemed strangely lacklustre, lacking the plumpness she associated with babies. But then, Callie thought doubtfully, she'd never really had much to do with babies. And other than that, the twins appeared untroubled by the chaos through which they had just travelled.

Remembering the blood stained knife Guidry had given her, Callie looked at her hand—but the knife was gone.

Guidry. Memories tumbled through her mind: Guidry giving her the knife that was now gone. Guidry only days earlier, making her repeat a Paris address, then only moments ago standing before her and roaring, *Rue Vivienne. Remember, Callie!*

But had it been only moments ago?

Hearing two male voices coming, Callie shrank back into a shadowed alcove between two buildings, her heart thudding. The two men were wearing odd red caps that looked a little like socks, the conical ends hanging over to one side. *"Oui,"* one murmured to the other as they neared Callie's hiding spot. *"Le Comte et sa fille, ils sont partis."*

Mentally translating the French, Callie looked around nervously for the Count and his daughter the two men were speaking of. Just as she realized how odd it was to be speaking of a Count at all, the man's companion said: *"Le Comte es avec Guidry? Tu es sûr?"*

The Count is with Guidry? You are sure?

Callie froze, holding her breath as the men passed where she was standing. *That can't be a coincidence,* she thought. *The men must be speaking of the same Guidry.*

"Oui, et même maintenant en route pour l'Angleterre." Yes, and even now on their way to England.

The men passed Callie without seeing her, their low voices fading into the distance, leaving her tingling with excitement and fear.

A Count. Guidry.

She looked down at her feet, and realised the smooth, hard surface she had felt beneath her face was, in fact, a cobblestoned street. The glow was not the steady glow of electricity, but the low yellow of an oil lamp.

The men were not wearing odd hats, Callie thought, with mingled fear and excitement. They were wearing the phrygian caps of the sans culottes, the French revolutionaries. The lamps above weren't dull yellow by design; they weren't electric lamps at all. They were oil lanterns. And that distant, hollow rapping wasn't some kind of building work. It was horse hooves striking the cobblestones. There was no scent of car exhaust, or traffic sounds. The stink she had noticed as she woke came from horse manure scattered across the street.

"I think I know where we are," Callie whispered. She looked down at where the twins stared back at her silently, through solemn blue eyes. She stepped out cautiously into the deserted street, moving toward the corner, where dark letters were carved into the stone: Rue Colbert.

Not Rue Vivienne, as she had thought.

Callie's heart sank. Then she recalled the story Guidry told her: *"Those of us who worked with Madame Lysette did not enter from the Rue Vivienne . . . There was another door, a tunnel, that came up into her cellar. The entry to that was through a knife maker's shop, in a nearby street."*

Glancing behind her, Callie saw a sign hanging in the shadows, right above where only moments ago she had been lying on the cobblestones.

M. Duval, Coutelier.

Coutelier. Callie searched her mental bank of French. *Knifemaker.*

An icy sensation trickled down Callie's spine. Cautiously she peered around the corner of Rue Colbert. Sure enough, there was a street name carved on the stone there, too: Rue Vivienne.

Callie was gripped by a queer thrill at the same time that a rising draught wafted the alley stench over her. Callie wrinkled her nose in distaste, then froze.

That sharp metallic scent that felt like danger wasn't just waste.

It was blood.

She peered down Rue Vivienne, heart pounding, praying that nobody would come across her. Down the street she could see another sign, lit by the soft red lantern above the door. On it was a single, red rose.

La Rose.

"We are in Paris," whispered Callie. She needed to say it aloud. Looking down at the twin sets of blue eyes, she said, "but you already knew that, didn't you?" The twins watched her solemnly, but still made no sound. Callie looked about her with dawning wonder. "And if I am right, and Guidry made me repeat that address for just this moment, then we are in the 2nd Arrondissement, in a place called Filles-Saint-Thomas."A printed paper blew by on the street. Picking it up, Callie scanned the French words. It was no more than a crude cartoon with a brief one line message, urging fellow revolutionaries to join a meeting that night, and adding a location.

But it wasn't the words or cartoon that interested Callie. It was the date.

The 20th of October, 1793.

The twins had brought Callie Lafayette through time to the bloodiest, most dangerous period of the French Revolution, known to history by two simple, horrifying words: *La Terreur*.

The Terror.

Heart thudding, babies held close to her chest, Callie was seized by a sudden sense of foreboding. Pulling back the swaddling on the infants, she felt her heart stop altogether.

The pendants were gone.

With increasing urgency she scrabbled through the cloth, her fingers searching every fold for the pendants she remembered placing on each baby as they were born, just as Guidry had instructed her to do.

But they had simply vanished, as cleanly as if they had never been.

With a sinking heart, Callie remembered the twins' sharp cry of loss as they fell through the dark chaos of time. *That was it*, she thought, with dull certainty. *They cried because they felt their pendants fall off in the darkness.*

Pendants that had been wrought by unknown hands and magic, and filled with an unknown combination of elements. Pendants which, Harper had told her, were the very means by which the twins found their way through time. Callie remembered Guidry's warning, only a day before the twins were born, to put the pendants on the twins the moment they were born. *They must never take them off, Callie.*

Had he known that she would find herself here, without the pendants? Had he warned her to put them on the twins for exactly that reason? Had he done all he could to prevent this exact problem, only for her to lose the pendants anyway, somewhere in the infinite mayhem from which Callie and the twins had just emerged? *Either way*, she thought, fighting for calm through a rising tide of panic, *now we are all lost in time—with no way of getting back.*

Callie knew there was no way to find the pendants again. Even if she had the faintest inkling of how to do it, the mere thought of voluntarily re-entering that dark madness terrified her beyond description. She looked down at the vial in her hand. It was quiet now, dull, with none of the pulsating force she had felt when it was near Harper, or as they tumbled through time. But perhaps, she thought, it was a connection to Harper.

Harper. Please tell me what to do. The pendants are lost, your babies are in danger, and I have no idea what to do.

But no answering voice came from the vial. There was no magical whisper, or sudden glowing against her skin. The vial was dull and silent. There was nothing but the dark night, and the scent of blood in the streets.

Clutching the tiny figures close, Callie drew a deep breath. Turning resolutely around, she headed for the sign reading *Monsieur Duval, Coutelier.*

FLEUR-DE-LIS CHAPTER 2

LA ROSE

Paris, 1793

The knifemaker stared at Callie. He had not moved throughout her story, his pale blue eyes watching her intently as she spoke, and even now that she had finished, still he did not move. Callie hadn't told him the whole. There were things, she discovered, that she could not say, words that simply choked in her throat. Antoine's name, for example, and Harper's. It wasn't that she didn't know the names; she did. But when she tried to verbalize them, the names simply would not come, and she knew that if she tried to write them, the pen would not form the letters. There were things about Guidry's role she could not quite explain, either. So the story was primarily her own. Not about Katiusca, or the Abatey; and certainly not about how Harper had turned into something else, something evil. She couldn't quite bring herself to tell that part of it. Instead, she had spoken of Keziah, of the threat the ancient vampire was to the twins, though again, she hadn't explained why, exactly, only that Keziah wanted to take them. She had, for a moment, thought of lying about how she had come to be there, in case the knifemaker didn't believe her. But his face was so kind, and his presence so quietly comforting, that once she had begun speaking, the words had just tumbled out. Now, however, as he simply stared at her without speaking, Callie began to feel uneasy. What if Monsieur Duval knew nothing of the kind of creatures she was talking about? Guidry had said that he made knives specifically designed to combat vampires. Monsieur Duval knew Guidry, and Guidry was a wolf. But perhaps he had not understood exactly what Guidry was, nor what the knives were for?

As all of this passed through Callie's mind, the babies still cradled in her arms began to stir, making weak, fretful sounds. Monsieur Duval looked down at them with the same rather horrified expression he had when she arrived.

"*Enfants*," he said, in much the same manner one might say, *dragons*. Standing up abruptly and slapping his thighs decisively, he nodded at the pantry behind him. "These, I know nothing of. We will go to Lysette, *oui*, and give to her *les enfants*, and there we shall see what is to be done."

"Lysette?" Callie felt her heart lift for the first time since she had woken on the cobblestones. "You mean Madame Lysette, of La Rose?"

The knifemaker frowned. "In this story you tell it is she whom Guidry told you to come and find, is it not?"

"It is not a story." A sense of hopelessness mingled with indignation made Callie's voice defiant. "I know how it sounds. But it is the truth. I'm not sure what it was that Guidry wished me to find, if I am honest, Monsieur Duval. I don't know what he knew. All I know is that he gave me your knife, and your name; made me memorize the address of La Rose, and told me the codename: Boucher."

"Pah!" Making an exasperated sound, the knifemaker opened the door to the pantry. Moving aside several heavy casks of brandy, he reached behind a large jar of pickled onions. There must have been a hidden handle of some kind, for a small door swung open, revealing a dark passage beyond. "We will wait for Lysette, who can generally find the truth. And you will stop calling me Monsieur, for it reminds me of my father, yes, and he was not a nice man. And you will tell me your own name, for I cannot take someone to Lysette without a name." He turned around, raising his eyebrows enquiringly, and Callie realised to her shock that she had not once mentioned who she actually was.

"I'm Callie. Callie Lafayette." Somehow, the name seemed odd, here, out of place. Callie felt as if it no longer truly belonged to her. She had a sudden recollection of selling her Mom's car, before she left Memphis. It had been part of her life from the day she was born, as familiar as the tiny, run down house she'd been raised in, or the sagging single bed she'd slept in since one of her Mom's many boyfriends had dragged it in off the street. But the moment Callie had signed the car over to it's new owner, she had truly seen it for the first time, as a stranger would: as just another car she might pass on the road, not a part of her. It had no longer felt like *hers*.

That was how Callie felt about her name, now. As if it didn't really belong to her. It was an odd, disconnected feeling, but she didn't have time to think on it over much, because Duval was gesturing impatiently at the passageway as he lit a candle and placed it in a glass case with a metal handle.

"*On y va! Vite!*" Let's go! Quickly!

Callie hastened to obey him, moving into the passage which was narrow and low enough that she had to stoop slightly, awkwardly balancing the babies, who were by now squirming and crying fretfully, in each arm. "Continue!" Duval said, waving her on, when she turned to check. He held the candle high over his head, and Callie groped her way in it's meagre light, unable to see more than a few feet ahead. It wasn't long before the tunnel came to a wooden door. "Now," Duval whispered behind her, "you tap three times, then pause, then three more, yes? And when they ask your name, you give them the name, Boucher, as you did with me, *oui?*"

"*Oui.*" Turning side on so she could knock without dropping the fretful infant in that arm, Callie tapped cautiously on the door, paused, and tapped again. There was a rustle on the other side of the door, then a low voice said, "*attend.*" Wait.

Callie heard the sound of footsteps retreating, and glanced back at Duval. "Now they fetch Lysette," he murmured. "It is the kitchen, you understand. The woman who works there, Jeanne, she is trustworthy, but Lysette, she does not give anyone the names." He shrugged. "Such things should be a secret, non?" Callie supposed they should, but she had no more time to think, because the footsteps had returned, this time two sets. She heard another rustle, then a soft voice said, "*Qui es la?*"

Callie drew a breath. "*Boucher.*"

There was a pause. Then: "I do not know who you are searching for," said the voice in French, this time cool, calm, and clearly dismissive, "but there is nobody by that name here."

Duval tsked in disapproval behind Callie. "She thinks you are an imposter," he said. "Lysette!" He put his head close to the door. "*C'est moi. Le Fer,*" he said clearly. "The Blade," he said, seeing Callie's brow furrow. He shrugged, slightly shamefacedly. "We were drunk when we think of these names, you must understand."

Callie found herself biting back unexpected laughter, and was still smiling when the door swung open to reveal a small room with an oven against one wall and a wooden bench at the centre. In front of it stood one of the prettiest, and tiniest, women Callie had ever seen. She had golden ringlets dressed high on her head, and sparkling cornflower blue eyes framed by wide, long lashes. Her skin was delicate as porcelain, with a soft blush in her cheeks, and her breasts swelled invitingly above a low cut gown. With her perfect red bow of a mouth and slightly arch look, she was, Callie, thought admiringly, exactly what she would have imagined an 18th century prostitute to look like, if she had ever thought to imagine such a thing.

She was also, quite unmistakably, to Callie's experienced eye, a vampire.

It was partly the odd shimmer of colour lurking just behind the cornflower blue surface of her eyes, like an oil slick on water. Partly the perfect, utterly unlined skin, and very white teeth. But most of all, it was the way Lysette froze as Callie emerged from the passageway, so utterly still she seemed, for a moment, like a perfect marble statue.

"Do not be alarmed, Lysette," Duval said from behind Callie, in French. "Our friend Guidry sent this one to us. But we will speak in English," he said, switching languages, "so she can understand. Her name is Callie," he added, and again Callie had the oddly disjointed feeling at hearing the name.

"I can speak French, if it is easier," she said, looking between them.

Duval rolled his eyes. "But, *non*. Your accent, it is not terrible, but it is also not good, and French, she should only be spoken by *Les Francaises*, who understand her properly." He nodded at Lysette, who had still not moved, other than to narrow her eyes slightly as she looked Callie up and down. "Lysette," Duval said impatiently, "As good as Jeanne's cooking is, I do not wish to stand in this kitchen all night. Take us somewhere we will not be overheard, and for goodness sake, find someone to feed *les enfants*, and quickly, before I throw them both into the soup pot."

"*Enfants*." Lysette repeated the word slowly, staring at the tiny bundles that were now making their presence unmistakably known. "You bring *enfants* to my house, Duval? And a girl who is dressing almost as badly as *les sans culottes* on the street? For what reason does Guidry send me such a creature? Jeanne," she called without waiting for an answer. A rather plump lady with brown hair in a loose bun, a sweet face and, Callie thought, the saddest eyes Callie had ever seen, came into the kitchen. Her eyes fell on to the small figures in Callie's arms, and flared with such longing, and grief, that Callie immediately guessed the cause of her sadness, especially when she came straight across the room and began to croon to the infants. Lifting one of them into her arms, she lowered the shoulder of her dress to reveal a full, heavy breast.

"Jeanne's baby died not two days ago," Lysette said. "She can feed these ones, I think."

Sure enough, the infant latched onto the breast, and a moment later, when Jeanne gestured to Callie to hand her the other baby, both drank quietly.

"What are their names?" Jeanne asked in French, not looking up from the two small heads as she sat on a stool in the corner.

"I don't know." In an instant, all that had happened, and the predicament she was in, rushed over Callie in a wave of exhaustion that was made no easier by watching Harper's babies drinking from someone else. *How is it that I don't know their names?* Callie searched her memory for any mention of what Harper had planned to call her babies, but could recall none. *We were all so worried about the night of her transition, about what she would become. When I thought of the babies, I thought about their abilities,* what *they may be; not about* who *they might be.* Now, as their sole guardian and the only link to the life they had come from, Callie felt an overwhelming sense of her own inadequacy to the situation they were in. "How will I get back," she whispered, staring at the two small heads. "How am I supposed to get them home?"

There was a moment's silence during which Callie was aware of Lysette and Duval exchanging a silent glance which must have served as some kind of code, for Lysette said briskly,"*Eh bien.* If Boucher sent you, then you must come inside. *Mais vraiment,* I do not know what he is thinking to send me a new mother with two - *two!* - enfants. *Ce n'est pas drole*, and I am not amused. But you will come with me upstairs. It is not safe on the streets, *non*. There is much trouble, this night." She cast a bright eye at the twins, now contentedly drinking from Jeanne. "All now is well here with *les bebes*. And we will go together, and you will explain to me why it is that Guidry entrusts his secrets with a strange girl, yes, and one with *deux enfants* also."

She cast another look at Duval, who said, "it is a story, Lysette. *Vraiment*, a story indeed."

"*D'accord*. Then, we go." She led them up the stairs, still chattering. Seeing Callie halt uncomfortably, Lysette nodded at Jeanne and spoke in rapid French then turned to Callie. "Jeanne will come too. I think you do not like to be parted from the little ones, *non?*" Despite her brisk delivery, Lysette's tone was kind enough that Callie could only nod for the lump in her throat. "Now," Lysette continued in the same business-like manner, "we must pass through the salon of La Rose to get to my apartment."

Pushing open a door, she stepped through, and Callie followed.

*F*LEUR DE *L*YS, THE BRIDGING BOOK BETWEEN THE *N*IGHTGARDEN *Saga and Waterpaths, can be preordered here.*

Following is an excerpt from The Wolves of Bayou Lune, a serial available on Patreon.

THE WOLVES OF BAYOU LUNE

EPISODE ONE

THE WOLVES OF BAYOU LUNE

AVERY

Episode One

Bayou Lune was the last place Avery should have been on a Friday night. Lowering the window of the hatchback she turned onto the bridge spanning the river and let the fragrant Mississippi breeze blow redwood and magnolias into the car. Avery inhaled deeply and screwed up her nose. Magnolias reminded her of Harper, and tonight, all Avery wanted to do was run from her friends. Louisiana, she thought, inhaling eagerly as the hatchback crossed the centrepoint of the bridge, smelled different. Richer. Wilder.

More dangerous.

And tonight, Avery Fairweather, A grade student, cheerleader and perfect only daughter of John and Sally, craved danger.

Not just standard, bayou kegger, high school danger. No, Avery wanted something quite different. She wanted the kind of danger that wore cut off sleeves and old ripped denim. That never finished school and sure wasn't headed for college. The kind of danger that didn't care how good her grades were, or what her ten year plan was.

Most of all, Avery craved the kind of danger that could drown out the strange whispers in her head.

Bayou Lune rushed toward her in a heady, sensual wave. Her friend Harper's garden always smelled sweet and light, like a summer breeze. But the bayous were sensual, a lazy, deceptive scent beneath which lay a thousand secrets. Things lay hidden in the bayous that other people did not see. And lately, Avery had felt as if she was living in a world nobody else saw, not even Harper, who Avery knew was hiding something; or Cass, her oldest friend. She hit the steering wheel with an open hand, then looked around guiltily, before remembering that nobody could see her. Cass was one reason Avery was driving across the state line tonight, after lying to her parents that she was studying with Harper. The other reason was Harper's gorgeous, utterly unobtainable, brother, Connor.

The fact was, Avery thought, as she turned off the highway and took the dual lane backroad that led to Bayou Lune, she knew Connor was out of her league. Maybe she'd always known it. People thought that looking like Avery did, with her endless olive toned legs, waist length dark hair, sloping almond eyes and perfect features, she would have her pick of men. But the reality, Avery had learned long ago, was much different.

She caught sight of the unsealed side road hidden among the hanging Spanish moss and wrenched the steering wheel to the left, hitting the potholes hard enough to make the little hatchback bounce and judder.

The reality was uglier. It was the older men who came into her parent's pharmacy surreptitiously eyeing her like she was prime catch of the day served up for their delectation. The reality was boys from school who whispered as she passed but were way too intimidated to ask her out. The girls who whispered behind their hands as she passed and spread rumors that she'd slept with every boy in town and some others besides, though the rumors couldn't be further from the truth.

The reality was the revolting history teacher finding a reason to touch her every time he passed her desk, but never blatantly enough to warrant a complaint.

Bute harshest reality of all, Avery had discovered a few years ago when she was barely fourteen, was that being blessed with Avery's kind of natural beauty meant that any complaint she did make was immediately assumed to be her fault. Men, a school counsellor had sternly advised her, did not approach young girls like herself unless they thought their advances would be welcome. Perhaps Avery should consider longer skirts, or looser sweaters. Perhaps she shouldn't smile so widely or be so welcoming.

Maybe up in the big cities such a response would be condemned. But in her hometown of Deepwater Hollow, population no more than a thousand on a good day, there were rules to follow. Avery Fairweather might be a knockout in her cheerleading uniform, but she wasn't ever going to be homecoming queen. Some prejudices were too deep, and too old, to be gone in a generation of good behaviour. And no matter what her parents had achieved, Avery would always wear the stench of the bayous over the river they'd once come from, even if she'd barely seen the mud herself.

Ahead of her still water gleamed through the trees. Avery slowed to a halt and switched the engine and lights off. The summer night was hot and still, as if it was waiting for something. Off somewhere to her right came the faint murmur of voices, the clink of bottles, and the soft plucking of a guitar.

She could still go back. It wasn't too late to turn the car around and drive back over to the river. She could go to Harper's, after all.

Then she thought of Connor's vivid blue eyes cutting away from hers whenever she caught them. Sliding across to rest on

Cass. The warm, slightly awed look in them when he did, a look he masked immediately if he realized he was being watched. A look Avery had never, ever seen on his face when Connor looked her way.

All those men. All her supposedly potent sex appeal, that men simply couldn't resist; and the one man Avery truly wanted didn't even so much as notice her, not even when Avery flipped past him in her shortest skirts, and wore the kind of low cut top she had thrust to the back of her closet years earlier.

No, Connor simply didn't see her. And even if he did, he didn't want what he saw. Whether Cass knew it or not, it was her Connor wanted, and Avery figured it wouldn't be long until she was forced to watch that relationship unfold with the same corrosive jealousy she had felt after Harper had arrived at their school last term, and immediately captured the single-minded attention of Antoine Marigny.

Wherever he had disappeared to.

Shaking her head impatiently, Avery gripped the steering wheel and stared ahead at where the moon gleamed off the bayou water.

Bayou Lune was different. The people here were hers, however far back in history their connection had been lost. Avery had Natchez blood, and the close-knit families of Bayou Lune were rumored to be descended from the same people. Her parents hated the Bayou families. Avery had relatives amongst them, she knew, but if she asked questions, all her parents would say stiffly was that they had worked their whole lives to be free of that life, and that Avery should be grateful she was growing up in a white painted house in Deepwater Hollow, instead of a rundown shack in the swamps. Family history was like the bayous themselves: hidden and mysterious. Avery knew better than to stir those waters at her parents' clean, scrubbed kitchen table.

Until one day last week, when Remy Thibodeaux had turned up in the pharmacy when her parents were out for lunch.

One wicked grin, a long, assessing look up and down her body from his gleaming topaz eyes, and Avery had felt something stir inside her that was more dangerous by far than any girlish crush on Connor Ellory.

"So." Remy had lounged across the counter, carved biceps smooth under the ripped sleeves of his flannel shirt, "What's a bayou girl like you doing in a white man's shop?"

It was the first time a stranger had ever directly acknowledged Avery's heritage. "How do you know where I'm from?"

He'd grinned. "Ain't too hard to work out, sweetheart. I been around faces like yours all my life." One calloused finger had stroked her cheek, and suddenly Avery couldn't move, could barely breathe. "Though," he went on, his voice lower, sultry, his eyes suddenly darkly serious, "ain't sure I've ever seen one quite so fine as yours."

The moment had been shattered by the bell clanging at the door and sudden return of Avery's parents, who had glared at Remy with such icy hostility that he'd straightened up and grinned at Avery.

"Well, best be off." He winked at her. "See you round, beautiful. Ma'am." He doffed an imaginary cap to Avery's parents with exaggerated courtesy. "Sir."

Then he left, and Avery had shrugged and brushed off her parents enquiries, grateful that her tawny skin hid blushes well, and that she was long practiced in hiding her emotions.

It was only when she put the cash in the register that she'd seen the note bundled up inside them.

Just his name, Remy Thibodeaux, and directions to a place in Bayou Lune. Tonight, at seven.

Avery took a deep breath and let go of the steering wheel. She'd spent all week wondering if she should come. Now that she was finally here, was she just going to sit in the car, like the good girl she'd been raised to be - or was she going to step out, into the darkness?

Pushing open the car door, Avery closed it firmly behind her. Without looking back, she moved forward into the trees, and the bayou hidden beyond.

THE WOLVES OF BAYOU LUNE WILL RUN AS AN ONGOING SERIAL on Patreon for subscribers only. Follow me there for updates. I am super excited about the Bayou Wolves! I've been writing it in the background but felt the story was too big for just a spin off, so I have started Avery's story at the beginning, and plan to build it over time until she ultimately gets her own series . . . after the next two series I have already planned. Please go to Patreon to follow the Wolves. https://www. patreon.com/Fehupress

AFTERWORD

There is plenty still to come in the Nightgarden Universe.

First I am releasing three bundles. Each will have bonus scenes and exclusive content. The final bundle, scheduled for release in June 2022, will also contain Fleur-de-Lis, Jeremiah and Callie's story. In the meantime you can read it on Patreon - the link is below, but will be taken down after publication of the bundle.

The Waterpaths Saga launches in September 2022 and consists of two trilogies, one for each twin. These books will also feature the characters you already know and love . . . and introduce some new ones, some you have heard of, some totally new.

I am writing the Wolves of Bayou Lune in the meantime so that you don't have hard withdrawal from the Nightgarden Saga! I will publish two episodes weekly on Patreon indefinitely, so you can go and sign up to that right away here. https://www.patreon.com/Fehupress

Finally, thank you for reading all this way. If you haven't already signed up to my mailing list, here is the link.

https://mailchi.mp/paulaconstant/nightgardenseries

ABOUT THE AUTHOR

Lucy Holden is the name under which author Paula Constant writes paranormal romance.

What began as a fun 'side hack' series has turned into an entire universe, and you can expect to see a lot more from Lucy Holden.

Paula lives in Broome, north west Australia, and loves dreaming on the beach under a full moon.

She is also the author of historical fiction series The Visigoths of Spain, and of travel memoirs Slow Journey South, and Sahara.

www.ingramcontent.com/pod-product-compliance
Lightning Source LLC
Chambersburg PA
CBHW010542170726
48285CB00008B/2715